Slocum dived for the st[...] any purchase. Inch by i[...] He wanted to have words with Old Pete about his leaving him and Helen Murchison stranded. Then he realized someone other than Old Pete was driving.

On hands and knees, Slocum made his way forward. He was reaching for his six-shooter when they hit a chuckhole. He made a noise that the new driver heard.

"We got company!" the driver shouted. "Behind me. On the roof!"

"Damnation!" came the curse from inside the coach. Then Slocum was weaving and dodging as bullet after bullet ripped through the wood under him. He rolled back onto his belly, felt a splinter dig into his chest, then slid forward enough to grab the driver around the neck. He tried to break it with a quick wrench but failed. His hands slipped off the man's sweaty skin.

"He's tryin' to stop me. Get him!" shouted the driver.

DON'T MISS THESE
ALL-ACTION WESTERN SERIES
FROM THE BERKLEY PUBLISHING GROUP

THE GUNSMITH by J. R. Roberts

Clint Adams was a legend among lawmen, outlaws, and ladies. They called him . . . the Gunsmith.

LONGARM by Tabor Evans

The popular long-running series about Deputy U.S. Marshal Long—his life, his loves, his fight for justice.

SLOCUM by Jake Logan

Today's longest-running action Western. John Slocum rides a deadly trail of hot blood and cold steel.

BUSHWHACKERS by B. J. Lanagan

An action-packed series by the creators of Longarm! The rousing adventures of the most brutal gang of cutthroats ever assembled—Quantrill's Raiders.

DIAMONDBACK by Guy Brewer

Dex Yancey is Diamondback, a Southern gentleman turned con man when his brother cheats him out of the family fortune. Ladies love him. Gamblers hate him. But nobody pulls one over on Dex . . .

WILDGUN by Jack Hanson

The blazing adventures of mountain man Will Barlow—from the creators of Longarm!

TEXAS TRACKER by Tom Calhoun

Meet J. T. Law: the most relentless—and dangerous— manhunter in all Texas. Where sheriffs and posses fail, he's the best man to bring in the most vicious outlaws—for a price.

JAKE LOGAN

SLOCUM
AND THE
TREASURE CHEST

JUVE BOOKS, NEW YORK

This is a work of fiction. Names, characters, places, and incidents either are the product of the author's imagination or are used fictitiously, and any resemblance to actual persons, living or dead, business establishments, events, or locales is entirely coincidental.

SLOCUM AND THE TREASURE CHEST

A Jove Book / published by arrangement with the author

PRINTING HISTORY
Jove edition / April 2003

Copyright © 2003 by Penguin Putnam Inc.

ISBN: 0-515-13512-7

A JOVE BOOK®
Jove Books are published by The Berkley Publishing Group,
a division of Penguin Putnam Inc.,
375 Hudson Street, New York, New York 10014.
JOVE and the "J" design
are trademarks belonging to Penguin Putnam Inc.

PRINTED IN THE UNITED STATES OF AMERICA

10 9 8 7 6 5 4 3 2 1

1

John Slocum was drifting off to sleep when the slow rocking of the stagecoach turned to sharp jolts as the driver hit every pothole and jagged rock in the rough Utah road. Slocum shifted his weight and almost fell out of the driver's box. He grabbed wildly and clung to the iron rail at his elbow as he righted himself.

"You missed one," Slocum complained to Old Pete.

The driver spat, the gooey brown quid arching into the air, only to curl back in the arid summer wind. Slocum wondered if it spattered against the side of the coach and got on any of the passengers. Two of them, the tinker and the snake oil salesman, would hardly notice, but the lovely young lady riding with them shouldn't have to endure such indignity. The trip was rugged enough without adding flying wads of chewing tobacco.

"What'd I miss? I don't miss nuthin', Slocum. You know that." Old Pete spat again, the gob this time hitting a rock alongside the road, where it sizzled in the hot early afternoon sun. Before Slocum could peer around and see if any of the brown tobacco juice ran down the side of the stage, Old Pete stood on the brake and snapped the reins hard to get them around a sharp bend in the road.

"A hole. You missed a pothole. You've hit every other one in the damned road."

"You surely are picky for a shotgun messenger, boy. Mostly, the ones they stick me with jist sit and don't say a goldurned word. Wish you'd do that 'stead of complainin' 'bout your precious lily-white butt bein' bounced around. We got time to make up if we want to get to the depot anytime soon."

Old Pete let off on the brake and cracked the long whip to get the six-horse team pulling hard up a rocky incline. Slocum wondered if the grizzled driver wanted to kill the animals, then saw how experience trumped caution. The stagecoach eventually rumbled to the crest of the steep hill. If Old Pete hadn't whipped the team to full effort, they might never have gotten to the top.

Slocum shifted his feet and rested his boots on the strongbox to better brace himself for the sudden plunge down the other side of the hill. The box was securely chained to the coach, but a canvas bag filled with mail slipped and slid around freely. He wanted to reach down to moor it, but the reckless driving made that dangerous.

"When will we get into Moab?" Slocum asked. He squinted at the sun and tried to guess at the time. They drove down the middle of a high-walled canyon that not only held in the heat but also robbed the day of a couple hours of sunlight. They'd be driving in darkness within the hour unless they got out of the canyon soon.

"Don't worry your head none 'bout that, Slocum. Drivin's my job. First the way station to swap out the team, then Moab. Call it another hour, but not much more'n that."

Slocum tugged at his hat as a blast-furnace-hot gust of wind caught him across his face. He held on to the floppy brim of the black hat to shield his eyes as he studied the terrain. He sat a mite straighter in the box when his sharp green eyes spotted something out of the ordinary.

"You see that?" Slocum asked, pointing toward the canyon rim.

"Didn't see nuthin'."

"Somebody with a signal mirror's up there," Slocum said.

"Your imagination's danged near as keen as your complainin'," Old Pete said in disgust. He fumbled in his pocket, got out another plug of tobacco and bit it in half. Hesitating a moment, he thrust out what remained to see if Slocum wanted to chew.

Slocum was too intent on the distant rim and what that flash of sunlight meant. He had spent his life alert for such warnings and knew the difference between sun shining on a gun barrel, off metal debris—and from a signal mirror. He craned his head around to study their back trail. The stage kicked up a powerful cloud of choking brown dust, obscuring the road. Without even knowing it, he reached down and touched the hot metal barrel of the shotgun pressing against his thigh.

"What's got you all riled?" Old Pete asked. "A flash of light and you get all flighty on me. Never had you pegged as someone with a nervous disposition. Maybe you ought to climb back and see if that peddler's got some tonic to settle your nerves." Old Pete coughed, spat and added, "I could use a swig, if he does."

"Don't need liquor," Slocum said. He leaned far out from the side of the stagecoach when Old Pete took another turn at breakneck speed. He caught a momentary glimpse of the road they had rumbled across a few minutes earlier, but he saw nothing amid the dust cloud to worry about. They were as alone as a whore at a church social.

But Slocum had heard rumors of Crow war parties in the area, come down from Montana to escape their reservation. He never put much stock in gossip, but settlers were beginning to disappear, their homes burned out.

"Suit yerself," Old Pete said. "I need somethin' to wet my whistle. The horses do, too."

"You give them whiskey?"

Old Pete laughed uproariously. "You got imagination and a sense of humor. Who'd have thought it of you, Slocum? You keep to yourself too much. Hell no, there's a spring 'bout a mile ahead where I kin let the horses drink their fill. Might even sample a bit of the water myself, if'n the peddler's not got any good nerve medicine in his case."

Slocum swiveled about often in the driver's box, hunting for signs they were riding into an ambush. He saw nothing. He finally began wondering if he was imagining danger to justify his job. He had ridden as shotgun guard for Wells Fargo more than a month and hadn't seen hide nor hair of trouble. Other stages had been attacked by a gang of road agents but Slocum's trips had been downright boring. As far as he was concerned, that was good and kept the fussbudget Wells Fargo agent in Moab, Gus Riordan, happy.

"What's in the strongbox?" he asked, trying to judge what their danger might be.

"Nuthin' to git antsy over, Slocum. We never carry gold or silver on this leg of the route."

"Then what's in the box?"

Old Pete shrugged. "Might be some Injun out there wantin' to steal the mail and read all the love letters. Them miners kin get purty detailed 'bout what they want to do, and I heard tell their sweethearts write back with even more particulars." He thought this was funny and laughed until he choked on the tobacco juice. Old Pete spat, then cursed a blue streak as the lead horses began faltering.

Slocum grabbed the iron rail at his side again as Old Pete stood, braced his feet against the front of the box and then pulled powerfully to bring the horses under control. They slowed and soon were walking, struggling to pull the heavy Concord coach over the rough road.

"Cain't keep 'em doing this long. When they get to runnin', it's easier for them to pull but they peter out quick in this heat. There's the waterin' hole." Old Pete jerked on the left reins and turned the team, getting off the road and heading for the pool of clear water visible from the driver's box.

Slocum felt a powerful thirst but waited until Old Pete had secured the brake and fastened the reins around the handle before climbing down. The canvas curtains inside the coach stirred a bit, showing that at least one of the passengers was still alive in the stifling hot box. The two men were the least of Slocum's worries. He opened the door to a burst of trapped heat, then poked his head inside.

"All out for a rest. Watering hole." He looked up at the woman, who sat closest to the door, and smiled. She was about the prettiest filly he had seen in months. The Mormon women in Moab all were taken, several of them sometimes by one man, and the whores in the saloons were uglier than mud fences.

But this woman was fair of face, graced with long dark hair and shining eyes the color of unfenced, endless blue sky. She moved gracefully, especially when she walked. Slocum would have had to have been blind—dead!—to have missed the long slender legs seductively hidden by her flaring skirts, and the hitch in her git-along as she moved.

A gust of wind caught the hem of the woman's calico dress and lifted it enough to give Slocum a glimpse of calf above the soft leather shoe that came to the top of her ankles. All in all, a pretty package to be delivering.

"Let me help you, ma'am," he offered, extending his hand. She took his calloused paw. He felt silky smooth flesh. She was a lady born and bred to the manor. With a swish of her long skirts, she stepped to the edge of the compartment, where Slocum was able to guide her to the ground. She floated like a feather.

"Thank you, sir," she said, gracing him with a boldly appraising stare.

"Slocum, ma'am, John Slocum." He touched the brim of his hat.

"Helen Murchison," she responded, giving him a smile that was more than friendly. Slocum tried to brush it off as a product of that active imagination Old Pete had accused him of having, but when Helen didn't remove her hand from his right away, he knew he wasn't suffering from delusion brought on by sunstroke and dehydration.

"You gonna get out of the way so we can get to the water?" asked the tinker. The man looked like a bulldog about ready to bite.

"Your nerves are frazzled from the rough trip, sir," the peddler said. "I told you to sample a bit of Dr. Dayton's Nerve Restorative. Fifty cents the bottle and—"

"Shaddup," the tinker said, swinging out of the compartment, hitting the ground hard and then stomping off to where Old Pete already watered the team.

"A most disagreeable man," the snake oil salesman said. He shrugged it off. "Your company more than makes up for his unpleasant behavior, Miss Murchison." With that, the peddler went to a different spot along the shore of the pond and knelt, taking out an empty bottle from his case and filling it so he could test the waters without getting his plain black broadcloth coat muddy.

"Are you going to drink, also, Mr. Slocum?" the dark-haired woman asked.

"Of course. It gets mighty dusty up in the box."

"And inside," she said, glancing back at the Concord's passenger compartment. She hesitated, as if wanting to say more to him, then turned and went to the pond. Slocum would have walked with her, but the view from the back was more pleasing.

Helen instinctively knew why he let her precede him and gave her bustle a twitch and a roll, just to keep him following.

Slocum drank quickly. When he finished he noticed that Helen was watching him out of the corner of her eye. She turned and smiled that daylight-bright smile of hers.

"Will we leave soon?" she asked.

Slocum saw that Old Pete was letting the horses rest before leading them to the pond for a final drink. Having the animals drink too much too fast and bloat was the last thing any of them wanted. They might be within a few hours of the last way station outside of Moab, but the canyon was mighty desolate.

"A half hour, maybe," he said.

"Then there is time for us to get to know one another better," Helen said.

"Nothing could please me more, Miss Murchison—"

"Helen," she insisted.

Slocum cast a glance at the other men. It wouldn't do for him to call this young lady by her given name in front of them. He didn't want to besmirch her reputation.

"I'd like nothing better, Helen, but I want to walk a ways back down the road."

"Oh?" she asked, her eyebrows arching slightly. "Did something fall off the coach?"

"No," Slocum said. "Old Pete thinks I'm being overly cautious, but I've learned to respect my gut feelings. Right now, I'm a tad uneasy about being out here."

"Should I worry?" Helen asked, her slender-fingered hand going to her full lips in a gesture of mock concern. Then she laughed. "Of course not, as long as I'm with you. Allow me to accompany you on this small trek of yours."

"That's a bad idea," Slocum said, not knowing what he would find.

"Nonsense. I can use the exercise. I need to stretch my

legs after being cooped up in that tight, hot sweatbox all day long."

"What would they think?" Slocum glanced in the direction of the other passengers.

"Who cares? I certainly do not. They are disagreeable in the extreme. The tinker does nothing but complain and Dr. Dayton goes on and on about horrid debilitating diseases and how his concoction can cure them." Helen moved closer and said in a conspiratorial whisper, "His medicine is nothing more than cheap whiskey, I am sure."

"I'm sure you're right," Slocum said.

"You wouldn't get in trouble with your boss if I came along?" she asked guilelessly.

"Old Pete's not my boss."

"I didn't think so. Then let's be off. The sooner we go, the sooner we can return to finish the trip."

"Pete!" Slocum shouted. "I'm going to see if anyone's following us. Be back in twenty minutes."

He didn't hear what Old Pete answered, but when the driver saw Helen accompanying him he grumbled under his breath until Slocum and the woman were out of earshot.

"My, he certainly knows a passel of colorful words, doesn't he?" Helen laughed delightedly. Then she quieted when she saw how Slocum took the leather thong off the hammer of the Colt Navy slung in his cross-draw holster.

"Don't worry about it," Slocum said. "Old Pete's probably right about me being too antsy."

"What are you looking for?" Helen asked, brushing a vagrant strand of her midnight dark hair from her eyes.

Slocum wanted to answer, *Danger,* but instead said, "I want to be sure whoever's coming up behind us isn't in any trouble."

"There's someone else on the trail?" Helen shrugged. "I hate being cooped up inside that awful compartment, though it is worse keeping the curtains up and letting in all that dust."

"Travel can be something of a trial," Slocum allowed, hardly paying the lovely woman any attention as he reached the point in the road where the dust had begun to settle. He wiped his eyes clear of grit, then studied the road for any hint that the mirror signal he had seen had alerted a band of road agents to come after them.

"May I help in some way?" Helen asked. She stepped closer, her warmth stirring Slocum. He moved away from her. "Oh, was it something I said? I know. I haven't had a bath in almost a week. That's it, though you are hardly any more fastidious."

"I've got a job to do, and that's keeping you and the stage safe," Slocum said. "When we get to Moab, might be I can buy you dinner. There're not many decent restaurants there, but one place out to the north of town's not likely to poison us."

"I do accept, John," Helen said. "And after we've dined . . ." Helen's words trailed off and she frowned.

Slocum heard the unusual sounds the same time she did.

"The stagecoach," he cried. "Stay here!" He hadn't taken a half dozen long strides when the gunshots rang out. Three came almost as one, then a half dozen more followed, mingled with the loud neighing of the horses. Slocum broke into a run in time to see the stage rolling from side to side as it struggled to get up enough momentum to take the next hill in the road.

He glanced toward the watering hole and saw nothing worth stopping for. Digging his toes in, he sprinted after the departing stage. Slocum wanted to call out to Old Pete but his breath came in ragged gasps. Doggedly chasing after the coach, he got within a few feet as it reached the summit of the hill. He had to act fast.

Slocum dived forward, his fingers groping for any purchase. His left hand caught a rope dangling from the boot as the stagecoach began its downhill plunge. Slocum was dragged along for a few yards, then got his feet under him and lunged forward, grabbing the canvas covering over the passengers' luggage. Inch by inch he pulled himself up until he could turn around and sit on the edge of the boot.

The stage kicked up a constant cloud of blinding dust, making breathing hard. Slocum pulled up his bandanna, then began the climb to the top of the coach. He wanted to have words with Old Pete about stranding him and Helen Murchison like he had.

Rolling over onto the top of the stage put Slocum into position to see the back of the driver's head. He went cold inside when he realized someone other than Old Pete was driving.

On hands and knees, Slocum made his way forward. He was reaching for his six-shooter to order the road agent driving the stage to halt when they hit a chuckhole. He made a wild grab to keep from being thrown off the roof and caused a commotion that brought the driver around.

"We got company!" the driver shouted. "Behind me. On the roof!"

"Damnation!" came the curse from inside the compartment. Then Slocum was weaving and dodging as bullet after bullet ripped through the wood under him. From the amount of lead splintering the roof all around him, he thought there had to be at least two more bandits inside.

Slocum rolled back onto his belly, felt a splinter dig into his chest, then slid forward enough to grab the driver around the neck. He tried to break the road agent's neck with a quick wrench but failed. His hands slipped off the man's sweaty skin.

"He's tryin' to stop me. Get him, get him!" shouted the driver.

Slocum swung clumsily and landed a weak punch to

the side of the desperado's head. The driver jerked from the blow, but Slocum was thrown off balance and slid to the far side of the roof, where hands reached up to grab hold of his boots.

"We got 'im!"

Slocum kicked one foot free, but the strong hands held his left boot. As they began tugging to pull him over the side, he tried to get out his six-gun again. This was his undoing. He released his grip to go for the gun and bounced up into the air.

Pressure on his foot, going airborne because of the rattling motion of the stagecoach, and not having a firm grip—all conspired against him. For a moment Slocum thought he had become a bird and taken flight. Then he realized he was sailing through the air. An instant later he hit the ground so hard it knocked the breath from his lungs.

By the time he sat up, painfully sucking wind into his tortured chest, the stagecoach was too far away for him to overtake.

A million thoughts raced through his head. The gunfire meant Old Pete and the two men passengers were probably dead. Otherwise, he would have seen them when he passed the water hole. Leaving Helen to fend for herself back on the road seemed a cruel thing to do, but she was safe if she stayed by the water. Sooner or later another stage would come by and take her on into Moab.

Slocum had a duty guarding the Wells Fargo coach and had done a piss-poor job of it so far today. He stood, brushed himself off, checked his ebony-handled Colt in its holster, then set out after the stolen stagecoach. It'd be a long walk to find it but when he did, the outlaws would pay dearly.

2

The sun silently slipped behind the high canyon walls and turned the desert cold before five o'clock. Slocum glanced at his watch, the only legacy from his brother Robert, then snapped shut the case and put it back into his vest pocket. He had been walking for over an hour and had yet to catch sight of the elusive stagecoach. As he hiked along the dusty road, he kept thinking about how he had left Helen alone.

If she found the bodies around the watering hole, she might become hysterical and need comforting. Slocum snorted in disgust. He was inventing reasons not to find the outlaws who had stolen the stage and bring them to justice. Wells Fargo had hired him to protect the passengers and valuables on the coach and he had failed. Helen would be all right, but the two passengers and Old Pete were probably dead. For them, all he could do was make certain their killers never robbed another stage—or took another breath.

Slocum sank to a rock and pulled off his left boot. He had worn blisters on his feet from so much walking. This made him even more determined to find the road agents and put a slug or two into their black hearts. His back hurt from the fall he had taken, but most of all a burning in his gut fired him to keep walking. He might give up, fetch Helen and see her into Moab, but then the robbers would likely get away scot-free.

Determined to do his job, he set out again along the road, and soon found where the stagecoach had taken a small side road that was hardly more than twin ruts in the desert. Slocum touched the butt of his six-shooter to make sure it rode easy and would come into his hand quickly if he needed it, then picked up the pace. When it got dark, it got dark fast in a canyon like this. He felt time slipping away as he tromped along on the trail.

It was past eight and darker than the bottom of a well when he came to a fork in the trail. Slocum dropped to his knees and studied the ground, but the dust didn't take prints easily and had been stirred up by twilight winds. Worse, the branching roads both led into diverging canyons. The roadbed itself was more rock than dirt, forcing him to look for scratches and other signs of horses' hooves breaking up rock.

Slocum walked a hundred yards up one canyon, then retraced his tracks and repeated the careful search along the second road. He hunted for horse dung, bright scratches in the rock—anything to show that the robbers had gone one way or the other. By the time the bright quarter moon shone down on him, he was nearing the end of his rope. Neither road appeared to have been traveled recently.

"Got to be one or the other," Slocum said. He was positive the stage had left the main road and come this way. But by which road? Slocum had a feeling that if he found the stage, he'd also find the road agents' camp. He might take the lot of them prisoner and get enough of a reward to move on. Riding on west appealed more and more to him. Maybe he would go to San Francisco, since he hadn't seen that fine city in a spell. Having a sizable wad of greenbacks in his shirt pocket was the best that could come out of this.

He began thinking on what the worst could be and decided not to get too aggressive going after the road agents—until he was certain he could take them all.

He shifted from foot to foot, painfully aware of the blisters, as he tried to choose between the two roads. Slocum finally spat on the back of his left hand, then slapped the gobbet with his right index finger. The spittle shot away like a frightened rabbit, going more to the left than the right.

Slocum hitched up his trousers and began walking in the direction already taken by the gob of spit. Without any trace plainly indicating one over the other, this seemed as easy a way of choosing as any. What became difficult quickly was walking in the darkness. The starlight was bright, and the moon helped him along his way, but on the ground it was still darker than the inside of a cow. More than once he twisted his ankle by stepping into a pothole. He began to appreciate what a four-legged horse went through pulling a stage along such stony roads. The slightest misstep could mean a broken leg.

The wind picked up and blew down the canyon against his face, chilling him after the long day's heat. He wished he had his duster, but that was aboard the stage. But on the wind came an earthy smell that kept him moving. A dozen yards farther down the road he found a pile of scat.

"Horse dung," he said, poking at it with a stick. "Fresh. And there's another pile." Slocum felt reinvigorated. His luck was holding. Several horses had come this way within the past few hours. They had to belong to the team pulling the stolen stagecoach. They just had to, or his entire hunt was for naught.

As he hurried along, he began worrying about the robbery a little more. Killing the driver and passengers was unusual, but taking the entire stage was downright peculiar. Search their victims, shoot open the strongbox, maybe steal the mailbag—but why take the entire stage?

A curious whistling alerted Slocum to something ahead. He looked around and shivered. The canyon pinched down to a narrow passage here, the twin ruts that passed for a road running smack down the middle. The soft red sandstone walls came in so close Slocum fancied he might reach out and touch both at the same time when he got to the narrowest point.

The whistle grew louder and then died with the wind. In the momentary calm, Slocum rushed forward, six-gun drawn and ready to fight. A huge dark shape loomed ahead, in the middle of the road like a crouching giant. As the wind kicked up again, the whistling sound returned.

Slocum got off the road and went along the canyon wall, its cold rock occasionally brushing his left shoulder as he made his way forward to a spot where he could see that the stagecoach stood abandoned on the road. Warily looking for the road agent, Slocum circled the coach, then went to it.

The wind gusted through bullet holes in the roof, causing the whistling sound that had alerted him. But the horses were gone and the passenger compartment was empty. Slocum pulled himself up into the driver's box and fumbled around. The strongbox had been taken, as well as the canvas mailbag. He sank back on the hard seat, considering what he ought to do next.

The outlaws had to have pressed on along the road or he would have run head-on into them. He swung around and made his way across the splintery top of the stage, remembering the last time he had been here. Men had shot at him from inside, and the jerky motion had finally thrown him off.

Slocum slid down the back of the stage and pushed back the canvas covering the passengers' luggage. He wasn't surprised when he found it all gone. The road agents had stolen everything, making Slocum wonder if there had been something in the baggage they had wanted even more than the strongbox and mail. That still didn't tell him why they had driven off with the entire stage. Kill the driver and passengers, root through their belongings at the water hole and then ride off. Even if the outlaws had wanted the team, too, there was no reason to steal the coach.

Slocum started walking again and found the spot where the outlaws had rummaged through the trunk and cases taken from the stagecoach boot. Clothes had been strewn everywhere. From what he could tell, they had taken all of the peddler's nerve tonic and nothing from the tinker's trunk. Slocum grew angrier by the minute when he found Helen's belongings. The highwaymen hadn't been happy with searching her trunk. They had shredded her clothing, then broken apart the trunk itself until only flinders were left.

In the back of his mind, Slocum had hoped to find Helen's possessions intact so he could use returning them as an excuse for seeing her again. He felt he needed some reason to speak with her after abandoning her the way he had. Still, he had almost stopped the robbers and had gotten a good look at the road agent who had driven the stage. Slocum was sure he could identify the man if he saw him again. Picking him off a wanted poster would be more difficult—pictures on such wanted posters were seldom more than crude sketches. This had saved Slocum's hide more than once, since he had not lived what could be called an unsullied life since coming out west from Georgia after the war.

In truth, the reason he had left Slocum's Stand had been a carpetbagger judge and his hired gun. The judge had taken a fancy to the fine pastureland and had intended to start a horse ranch. Through forgery and outright lies, claiming nonpayment of back taxes, the judge had seized land that had been in the Slocum family for generations. Slocum had told the crooked judge he had to come for the land himself.

The judge and his gunman had. And they remained on the land, in shallow graves near the springhouse. Slocum had mounted his horse and headed west, never looking back. That had been good, because the sounds behind him too often were bounty hunters intent on bringing a judge killer to justice.

Slocum started down the road, but his feet got the better of him, forcing him to return to the spot where the road agents had rifled through the passengers' belongings. Since the male passengers wouldn't need a shirt or trousers again, Slocum used strips from their clothes to bind his blistered feet, after using carbolic acid he found in the peddler's kit. The flesh burned like hellfire, but he knew he would be in better shape after he rested.

He drifted off to sleep, staring up at the impenetrable black-rock canyon walls and thinking about Helen—and avenging three deaths.

Slocum came awake with a start, sitting up and looking around. Without knowing it he had whipped out his six-shooter and he held it firmly in his grasp. The sun poked up over the eastern canyon wall, telling him it was later in the day than he usually slept. Checking his watch bore this out. It was almost eight.

But the warm sunlight on his face hadn't awakened him. The sound of horses and men joking had. Slocum winced as he pulled his boots on over his bandaged feet, vowing to buy a good horse and keep it fed, watered and happy. Then he rolled away from where he had slept amid the tangle of clothing and came to rest on his belly, covering the road with his six-shooter.

Two men came riding from the direction he had intended to go. Before he could order them to stop, two more showed up. Then Slocum caught a glint off one's chest.

"Sheriff!" he called, standing. "Sheriff!"

The lawman swung about in the saddle, going for the heavy Smith & Wesson at his hip.

"Whoa, hold on. It's me, Slocum. The shotgun messenger on the stage. I work for Gus Riordan."

"Who?"

"Riordan, the Wells Fargo agent in Moab."

"I ain't the sheriff. Name's Yarrow and I'm marshal in Moab."

Slocum hesitated. He had been returned to Moab three times after Riordan hired him, most of his time spent on the trail and at the other end of the stage line in Colorado. But he didn't recall ever seeing Yarrow before.

"I thought Beeman was the marshal," Slocum said, eyeing the three men with the self-proclaimed marshal. They didn't have badges pinned on their vests, but they didn't have the hard look of road agents, either.

"Beeman upped and left a week back when he heard about a silver strike over in Nevada," said one of the others. "Marv and Rafe and me, we're ridin' posse with Marshal Yarrow here."

"So you're the new lawman?" asked Slocum.

"What's going on? I ain't answerin' *your* questions. You got to answer mine. Where's the stage?"

"Robbed," Slocum said. "The road agents abandoned it not twenty yards farther along the road." The dip in the road almost completely hid the abandoned stagecoach.

"Now, that seems real queer, if you ask me," spoke up the one named as Rafe. "What was you and Old Pete doin' takin' this road?"

"The outlaws killed him and two passengers and stole the entire stagecoach. They took the horses and rummaged through the trunks and left the stage where you see it." Slocum pointed back down the road to where the huge

Concord stood silently like a buffalo waiting for a hunter to bring it down with a well-placed shot.

"Now, why'd they go and do a thing like that?" asked Yarrow.

"What are you doing out here, Marshal?" Slocum asked. He didn't have a good answer for the lawman's question and wanted to keep Yarrow focused on finding the road agents.

"Huntin' for a son of a bitch what murdered three fine, upstanding citizens," Yarrow said.

Slocum was caught flat-footed when he found himself staring down the barrels of four drawn and cocked six-guns. He grabbed some sky to keep them from shooting him then and there.

3

"You kin get mighty hungry in that cell, Slocum, if I think you're lyin'," Marshal Yarrow said. Slocum had taken a powerful dislike to the lawman since being brought in at gunpoint. "Yes, sir, if you don't start tellin' me what you done with the strongbox and everything in it, I might jist forget to feed you for a week!"

"I didn't steal anything, Marshal. I told you I was on the trail of the road agents who did. Why didn't you and the posse run into them? Those are mighty narrow canyons. Not much room for hiding out."

"Those canyons are like a rat's nest, Slocum. They go all over the place, wigglin' this way 'n' that. That's why I reckon I was 'bout the luckiest gent on the face of the earth to catch you so easy. What happened? Did your partners double-cross you? Or maybe you didn't have any partners. You jist upped and killed Old Pete and the passengers, then drove off."

"How'd you hear about the robbery?" Slocum asked. They had been over this before but Yarrow seemed oblivious to the simplest logic. Slocum felt he had to keep the lawman's simple mind on track or he would derail again.

"Miss Murchison rode in with a family comin' to town

to buy supplies, after she hiked all the way to the depot. She told me 'bout the robbery.''

"Then she also told you we were together on the back trail when the outlaws killed Pete and the others." Slocum might have been talking to a boulder for all the response he got. Yarrow was a witless man and refused to be confused with anything approaching the truth once he had made up his mind.

"You'll come round, Slocum, I know it. You've only been in that cell for a couple minutes. You'll tell me what you done with all that gold."

"What gold?" Slocum went cold inside. Yarrow had put the noose over his head by accusing him of killing the driver and two passengers. This tightened it around his neck by making sure no one would listen to him. Murder was one thing, stealing gold another.

The marshal sneered, then hurried from the small cell block into his office when the tiny bell attached to the outer door clanged. Slocum went to the bars and shook them as hard as he could. They weren't bars as much as they were two-inch-wide strips of metal. No matter how hard he worked, he couldn't even get the rivets to squeak. The metal strips circled up overhead and down on all four sides. He didn't doubt they went under the dirt floor of the jail, too.

"I want to see the varmint," Slocum heard from the office. He didn't hear Yarrow's reply, but considerable argument ensued, until finally he saw the short, bowlegged Wells Fargo agent come through the door and waddle toward him.

"Mr. Riordan," Slocum said. "I—"

"Shut yer tater trap, Slocum," Gus Riordan snapped. "Killin' Old Pete was bad, but you had to go and kill two passengers to boot. And you stole all that gold! To think I trusted you. Goes to show how wrong a soul can be."

"What gold?" Slocum was at the end of his patience.

"Pete said there wasn't anything worth mentioning in the strongbox."

"You were carryin' sixteen thousand dollars' worth of gold."

Slocum stared at the Wells Fargo agent for a moment. Gus Riordan looked a dozen years older than he had the last time Slocum had seen him, ten days earlier. The murders had to take a toll on him, but the owner of the gold was going to become a permanent thorn in Riordan's side until Wells Fargo made good on that theft.

"Why didn't you tell me? Did Old Pete even know?"

"He knew. He worked for the company more'n four years, and we trusted him."

"You didn't trust me, though," Slocum said coldly. "Why didn't you get a cavalry detachment to ride along as guard?"

"I should have but we decided to sneak it past the road agents. Make it look like a regular shipment rather than something special. Besides, the cavalry unit over at Grand Junction ain't up for escortin' gold these days, not with the Indians scalpin' and robbin' everywhere you turn."

"Your plan didn't work and three men died because of it," Slocum said.

"You're the one on the wrong side of the bars. Fess up, Slocum. Tell the marshal where you hid the gold. Killing passengers is bad, but maybe we can overlook that since they didn't seem to have family to speak up for them."

"I didn't kill them."

Riordan heaved a sigh and shook his head. "You're in a world of trouble, Slocum. Make it easy on all of us. Marshal Yarrow says there's not gonna be any trouble getting you convicted. That hurts, too, since I thought so highly of you."

"Whose gold was it?"

Riordan turned bloodshot eyes to Slocum, studying

him. The man's hand shook when he reached for a hand-
kerchief to wipe sweat off his baldpate.

"It belonged to the company. Wells Fargo was moving
the gold to Moab so we could expand."

Slocum had nothing more to say. Whether Riordan had
been at fault, or his superiors back in San Francisco, for
moving so much gold without adequate protection, he
couldn't say. It didn't matter who had made the error of
sending so much gold without a large armed escort. Men
had died and gold had been stolen.

And Slocum knew he was the scapegoat for all the
crimes.

Riordan swabbed more sweat and left, mumbling to
himself. The Wells Fargo agent had been gone only a few
minutes when Marshal Yarrow returned.

The lawman swaggered in, thumbs locked in his gun
belt. He stared at Slocum, as if his muddy brown eyes
could burn holes in his prisoner. Yarrow blinked and
looked away from Slocum's steely green-eyed gaze.

"You're in a world of trouble, Slocum," Yarrow said.
"I talked a bit to Mr. Riordan, and he's willing to look
the other way when it comes to charging you with gold
theft if you tell where you hid it."

Slocum wondered if Yarrow was downright stupid
thinking anyone would fall for this, or if something more
brewed. Even if he had stolen the gold, returning it to
Wells Fargo was not going to make the murder charges
go away.

"What's happened to Miss Murchison?" Slocum asked.
Helen was his only hope of providing an alibi for the
crime. If she would go to Riordan and tell him everything
that had happened, how she and Slocum had been together
when the robbery occurred, then there was a chance he
could get out of this steel cage.

When Slocum was on the other side of the bars, he
would find the real culprits lickety-split.

"I talked awhile to her when she got into town. Thass how I knowed there was a robbery. She came in with the Glendower family. Fine, God-fearin', upstandin' folks. They vouched for her."

"You thought Miss Murchison had shot and killed those three and stolen the stage?"

"Cain't be too careful when there's murder," Yarrow said proudly.

Slocum knew he had no chance of getting out of this cell by convincing Yarrow he was innocent. He judged the distance to the marshal and saw how cleverly the marshal stayed just beyond reach. Slocum doubted he could grab the man's gun or that it would do a whole lot of good even if he did. The man had left the keys to the cell back in the office. Even holding the marshal at gunpoint and forcing a deputy to fetch the keys didn't seem too promising. Yarrow was new at the job, and Slocum doubted many in Moab cared what happened to him.

"I want to speak to Miss Murchison."

"No way," Yarrow said. "Besides, I think she might have moved on. Haven't seen her around town."

"You've been out hunting for the road agents who actually robbed the stage!" Slocum fought to keep his anger in check. Talking to Yarrow wasn't half as satisfying as shouting at a rock wall. At least there was a chance an echo would come back from a wall.

"Yeah, right," Yarrow said, as if this hadn't occurred to him before. "I was out catchin' you."

"I'm a good tracker, Marshal," Slocum said. "Get your posse together, let's all go back to where you found the stage and I can follow the trail."

"To the gold?"

"The outlaws have a hideout somewhere. I can find it."

"You're askin' me to let you out of the cell so you can go find your own hideout?"

"Think of it as getting the gold back," Slocum said,

anger smoldering. He had to get out of the cell, and the marshal was his only ticket to freedom.

"Reckon you might be on to something. If'n you hid the gold, you might not be up to makin' a map, but you have to know where you put it, so you could lead us there."

"Something like that," Slocum said, seeing the marshal working over the problem. Yarrow's face brightened, and he slapped his thigh.

"I'll get the boys together, and we can fetch that gold back 'fore sundown!"

The marshal left Slocum stewing in his own juices, wondering if he was doing the right thing. Then he looked at the gray iron strips all around him and knew he had no choice.

Slocum kept glancing over his shoulder, but as lackadaisical as the marshal was, the three men in the posse were vigilant. He rode slowly, glad to be in the saddle again. His feet still smarted from the blisters, but the chance for vengeance burned hotter than any pain. Whoever the outlaws were, they had put Slocum into a stewpot of trouble. He wasn't the kind of man who tolerated that for long.

"It's gone," Slocum said, eyes narrowing as he studied the trail ahead. They had ridden from Moab, taking the same trail the marshal had before. This approach through the winding, treacherously tall-walled red-rock canyons brought them to the spot where the stagecoach had been abandoned. Slocum had kept a sharp eye out for signs of the road agents but hadn't seen anything.

Now the Concord coach itself was missing.

"What's gone?" asked Yarrow. The man took a deep swig from his canteen and choked. Slocum guessed the marshal had replaced water with whiskey. Riding in the hot sun and drinking nothing but tarantula juice wasn't a good idea, but in Yarrow's case, Slocum doubted anyone would notice any difference.

"The stage. This is where the outlaws left it," Slocum said. He saw the opened trunks and scattered clothing but nothing of the stagecoach. He stood in the stirrups to get a better look and was aware of Marv and Rafe putting their hands to their six-shooters. They were as alert as any posse he had ever seen.

"Might be Mr. Riordan came for it. That's one real valuable hunk of rolling stock," Yarrow said.

"Might be," Slocum replied, but he saw the signs that the stage had been hitched to a team and driven off the road, heading toward a narrow canyon mouth. It made no sense that the road agents had returned for the stage. They had nearly sixty pounds of gold. Why further burden themselves with the stage?

"Kindling," Yarrow said. "Could be the varmints stole it to break it up into kindling wood to stay warm." He wiped his forehead again and took another swig of whiskey.

"In the middle of summer, Marshal?" asked Rafe. He exchanged quick glances with his two partners. They smiled but kept from laughing. "Who'd want to buy a shot-up stagecoach?"

"Doubt it," Yarrow said, frowning as if he worked on something real hard. "You might have a point. Why bust up a perfectly good stage?"

"Could be the outlaws want to ransom it. Heard tell them damn things cost ten thousand dollars or more," Marv said. "Reckon Mr. Riordan'd pay that rather than having to order up a new one."

"He doesn't have two nickels left to rub together," Rafe said. "Not after this varmint stole the gold."

"I didn't take it," Slocum said tiredly. He wondered why anyone would take the coach. Marv had a decent idea, but Slocum had never heard of any road agent ransoming a stagecoach before. After the way the passenger compartment had been shot up, Riordan might think better of getting a new coach from Wells Fargo. His job was likely at an end, no matter what he did, if the gold wasn't recovered.

Yarrow perked up at the exchange.

"Take us to where you buried the loot, Slocum. That was why we brung you out here."

"I said I'd help you track the outlaws, Marshal," Slocum reminded him. "If the stage went that way, so will we."

"Marshal, that don't make much sense," Rafe said. "We're here for the gold, not the stagecoach. Let Riordan worry on that awhile. Marv and Jack and me, we're here to collect the reward for recovering the gold."

"I know, I know," Yarrow said. "You boys don't let me forget I cain't put you on the payroll. There's hardly enough money for my salary." Yarrow bent over and said to Slocum in a conspiratorial whisper, "The town's only payin' me twenty dollars along with room 'n' board. I get to sleep in a cell if there's no prisoner. If there is, I have to sleep at my desk."

Slocum wondered what had happened to the prior marshal, and if he had really gotten the silver bug. Outlaws might have paid him to leave so this dingbat could be hired. Crime would run rife in Moab until the citizens got fed up with it, but by then the crooks would have stolen a decent amount of loot.

Or it might just have been that no one else wanted the job.

Slocum put his heels to the flanks of his horse and trotted after the stagecoach. The deep ruts showed where the heavy coach had almost mired down a few times in the soft sand of arroyo bottoms, but mostly the desert floor was baked harder than rock. As he neared the jagged entrance into the canyon where the stage had been taken, he slowed and studied the high walls eroded by wind and turned into Swiss cheese. A half dozen snipers could be hidden in those cavities and he would never know until it was too late.

"Go on, Slocum, show us where you hid the gold," urged Yarrow.

"Ahead," Slocum said. Alongside the stagecoach tracks he saw hoofprints. At least four men had ridden near the stolen coach. As Slocum rode forward, he kept an eagle eye on the canyon rim and the myriad caves in the rocky faces rising sharply on either side. Less than a mile into the narrow canyon he spotted a small spring where a campfire had burned as recently as the morning.

He jumped from his horse and felt the ashes. Cold. But the rock beneath was warm, confirming his suspicion they hadn't missed the gang by more than a few hours.

"What's this, Slocum? Yer hideout?"

"It's where the road agents who stole the gold—and the stage—camped last night. I don't see any evidence they were here longer than that." He walked around the camp hunting for some clue where they might have gone. The tracks left by the stolen stagecoach remained his best chance for catching the desperadoes.

"Where do we dig?" asked Yarrow.

"Dig for what?" Slocum looked up at the marshal on his horse. He was aware of the lightness on his left hip where his Colt Navy usually hung. The marshal balanced a rifle in the crook of his left arm as he struggled to keep his horse under control. The muzzle pointed in Slocum's direction often enough to give him the message.

"Don't go funnin' me none, Slocum. The gold. Dig it up or I might jist leave your worthless carcass here for the coyotes."

"The outlaws pushed on, Marshal. They took the gold the day before and the stagecoach this morning." Slocum tried to make sense of it. The road agents had stolen the

gold and left the stagecoach, then had camped here overnight. When they had a good head start on any pursuit by
the law, they had returned to drive the stage back.

Slocum couldn't figure it out.

"Of course they left, you idiot," snapped Yarrow. "You
warned 'em. How many're in your gang?"

"We can overtake them," Slocum said, returning to his
horse. "They can't make very good speed along this rocky
canyon, not unless they leave the stagecoach behind. For
some reason, they want it as bad as they do the gold they
stole."

"So you're not gonna turn over the gold?"

Slocum stared up at the marshal and wondered what he
could say or do to make the man understand. From the
expression on the doltish man's face, Slocum knew the
answer was . . . nothing.

"We're goin' back to town," Marshal Yarrow declared.

"Without the gold?" whined Rafe.

"Without the damn gold but with the varmint what stole
it!" Yarrow motioned for Slocum to mount and head back
down the canyon, in the direction they had come.

4

Slocum tried to convince himself he wasn't any worse off than he had been before. It didn't work. He berated himself for not trying to make a break when he was in the winding maze of canyons outside Moab. He had been on horseback then, not on foot, and certainly not locked up in a jail cell nobody could escape. He could have gotten away from the dimwitted marshal even if the three unpaid deputies in his posse were alert for an escape attempt.

He had been out under the hot noonday sky where he belonged, not locked up inside a dingy metal-stripped cell, with only skill and cunning on his side. Slocum knew his chances of getting out of the jail cell had died to nothing when Marshal Yarrow locked the door behind him the last time.

Swinging his long legs around on the hard bunk, Slocum jumped up so he could look out the small window set in the rock wall just beyond the metal straps. A small knot of citizens gathered a dozen yards away in the side street. He wished he couldn't hear what they were saying.

"String him up!" shouted a florid man at the front of the slowly growing mob. "He killed three men! And he stole the gold!"

"You're just mad because you won't be working on the new depot, Bert," shouted another. "We all're going to hurt 'cause the stage company'll likely build their terminal somewhere else. But hanging the varmint in the jail won't get the gold back."

"He *killed* three men. To hell with the gold!"

This started an argument that caused a shiver to run down Slocum's spine on cold, prickly feet. He had seen the way mobs whipped themselves into a murdering frenzy. These men had been hurt in the wallet with the loss of the gold intended to build a new Wells Fargo depot. They didn't want to look greedy so they grabbed onto another excuse to vent their wrath. The road agents had killed three men, only one of whom might have been known to the Moab citizens. Somehow, Slocum doubted the presence of Old Pete had made much of a ripple in the local pond. The stage driver had been garrulous, obnoxious and more than a little ill-natured.

The mob wanted blood to soothe their loss, and it had nothing to do with justice or letting three men's souls rest easy.

"I got a rope. Who can tie a hangman's noose?"

A cry went up in the crowd as several men shoved through to hitch the knot that would break Slocum's neck. He watched as the hemp rope was tossed out and two men grabbed for it at the same, both eager to be in this necktie party. They were building up their courage to toss that rope over a tree limb and let Slocum swing until his boot heels stopped kicking.

"You boys—now, what're you up to?" came a familiar voice. Slocum slid to the far side of the small window and saw Marshal Yarrow trying to attract the mob's attention.

"Out of our way, Marshal. This ain't your fight. Let us bring justice to Moab, for a change. Ain't been justice here since Marshal Beeman left."

"There's always been justice here, Ned Dawkins," the

marshal said sternly, singling out the ringleader. "There's gonna be law and order to go with justice. You cain't string him up 'fore a judge and jury find him guilty. I admit, he *is* guilty as sin, but we gotta do things right. Trial first, then you can hang 'im as high as you like."

Slocum sagged when he heard Yarrow. The marshal told the strident rabble his prisoner was guilty and then egged them on to become a full-fledged lynch mob. He wondered if they would bring picnic baskets to the hanging so they could make a full holiday of it. Slocum didn't put it past the good people of Moab.

He dropped back to the dirt floor and began scuffing a hole. It was as he had guessed earlier. The broad metal straps crisscrossed under the floor, too. He was imprisoned and wasn't going to get out. The marshal might be a bit on the dim side, but the town had built a sturdy hoosegow for its prisoners.

Slocum began examining the ironwork inch by inch, only to give up when he got to the sturdy cell door. There wasn't a speck of rust anywhere, and this was as sturdy a cage as ever had been built. It was his bad luck to be on the wrong side of its door. He looked up to see Yarrow filling the doorway to the office with his considerable bulk.

"Slocum, you want to tell me what you done with the gold? I might be able to save you, though them folks outside are mighty hot under the collar. Cain't say I much blame 'em since the stagecoach company's makin' noises about going into Green River instead of here with their big regional depot. Tell me what I need to know so I kin keep them from doin' somethin' illegal to you." The marshal jerked his thumb over his shoulder, in the direction of the outer office and the street beyond. The increasingly noisy crowd had come around to the front of the jail, building up courage to storm in to seize their victim.

"I turn over the gold and you'll keep me safe? Is that it, Marshal?"

"Well, cain't rightly promise the judge won't hang you, but you'd go to your grave a mite easier knowin' Moab was secure with a new Wells Fargo office."

Slocum wanted to tell the marshal he had a great deal to learn about lying to prisoners to get confessions. He motioned the lawman closer, hoping to get the man's six-shooter. Yarrow had left the keys out in the office, so Slocum was in as bad a position as before, but with the six-gun he could take out a few of the crowd when they came to lynch him.

Yarrow stepped up and then froze when a shotgun blast sounded outside the jailhouse. He swung around and left Slocum grasping for the unprotected six-shooter in the marshal's holster. Slocum pressed his face against cold iron strap and then sagged. He had missed another chance. There had to be some other way out of the cell.

There had to be or he'd be dead before sundown.

A second shotgun blast echoed along the streets of Moab, then faded away until only a single voice could be heard.

"You have no right to string him up. You should be ashamed of yourselves. Go on, go home, or go to the saloon and get a drink. But go *somewhere*."

The outer door opened, and Slocum caught a glimpse of Helen Murchison's trim figure. She crossed the outer office to Yarrow's desk. From the cell, Slocum could hear but not see the lovely woman.

"Marshal, you ought to be ashamed of yourself letting those frightened men assemble into a mob. They could have taken the law into their own hands."

"Ain't much wrong with that," Yarrow said, not in the least contrite. "The judge'd have to come down from Salt Lake City. That might take a spell, so what's wrong with lettin' justice be served now instead of later?"

Slocum heard Helen's bitter denunciation of such thinking. She eventually softened her tone a little and said, "Let me talk with Mr. Slocum. Just for a moment."

"Well, all right, but you cain't take that scattergun with you."

Slocum heard a clank as the heavy-barreled weapon dropped to the desk; then he saw Helen come to the door leading into the cell block. For a moment, his heart almost stopped. She was a beautiful woman, but the way the light silhouetted her turned her into an angelic vision.

"Mr. Slocum," she said, "so good to see you again."

"Thanks for saving my hide. They were going to lynch me."

"And Marshal Yarrow wasn't doing much to slow their progress," Helen finished with some bitterness. "I tried to get you free on bail, but the marshal won't hear of it."

"He's not as stupid as he looks, then," Slocum said in a low voice. Helen's blue eyes fixed on him. She smiled slowly.

"You'd hightail it from Utah, wouldn't you?"

"As soon as I take care of unfinished business."

"What might that be?"

"Somebody stole the gold from under my nose. If I hadn't taken that little walk with you, I could have—"

"Died with Old Pete and the others," Helen said, finishing the sentence for him. Slocum saw that completing his thought was a bad habit of hers, but he wasn't going to call her out on it. "I want to thank you for suggesting I accompany you on that little excursion. Otherwise, I would have been murdered, also."

Slocum didn't remember it that way but said nothing. He heard a ring of truth in Helen's comment about trying to bail him out.

"I think," Helen went on, "you actually would try to recover the stolen gold. And you would also find the men who killed those three because it's a personal matter with you now. Letting the real murderers go is an affront to your honor that you will not bear. Yes, I think all that is true."

"I need to get out, and not end up dangling from a hangman's rope," Slocum said.

Before Helen could respond, Marshal Yarrow called, "You got to move on now, Missy. I should clap you into the next cell after you shot that scattergun of yours outside, but I kin be kind to somebody as purty as you."

"You ran off the crowd?" This confirmed what Slocum had suspected. It took someone with a steel spine to stand up to an angry crowd bent on hanging.

"I have many talents," Helen said softly. Her blue eyes twinkled. "Later, I'll be happy to show you my marksmanship . . . and other things."

She turned with a soft swish of her skirts and walked out, head high. As she left the jailhouse, Slocum saw how she carried the shotgun with authority. They were fools in the crowd for trying to cross such a determined woman.

Slocum sank back to the bunk and spent the rest of the afternoon concocting one plan after another for getting out of the cell. Nothing came to him. Even if he wrestled out the marshal's gun to force him to open the cell, the man had to disappear around the corner to pick up the keys that would open this infernal cage. Slocum might get a moment's pleasure out of plugging the marshal, but it would really serve no purpose since he'd still be locked up. He wasn't above shooting a man who needed it, but the marshal was only doing his duty, however ineptly.

He even considered the chance of using the six shots in the gun to blast off the cell lock. In his experience, Slocum had never seen this work with a metal door. Shooting the lock itself only jammed up the mechanism and made the situation more desperate.

The light outside dimmed and the cell cooled off fast in the twilight. Slocum was pulling the thin blanket up around his shoulders when the marshal came in, carrying a tray of food.

"Decided you ought to get some victuals," Yarrow said.

Slocum was glad the marshal hadn't decided to follow up on the threat to starve him to death. He needed to maintain his strength to fight off the lynch mob when they came back. And they would. They always came back.

"Stay where you're at so I kin push this into the cell." The marshal put the tray on the floor and shoved it through a small opening at floor level intended for such purposes. He stepped back fast, as if Slocum might strike like a rattler from across the cell. "You call me when you've finished. I got to get the plate back to Miz McKean fer cleanin'."

Slocum put the tray on the end of the bunk and uncovered it. The smell of decent food made his mouth water, but what he found under the thick slab of meat loaf made his eyes go wide. He slid out the key and wiped it on the napkin. Slocum glanced at the cell door and then at the food.

He ate ravenously before trying the key in the lock. It silently turned and the door swung wide.

He quickly stepped back into the cell, closed the door and relocked it.

"Marshal, I'm done," Slocum called. "You wanted to take the tray, didn't you?"

"Push it back the way it came," Yarrow said, warily standing a few feet back. Slocum did as he was told. Yarrow took the tray and left. Slocum heard the outer jailhouse door clang as the warning bell swung to and fro, then shut decisively.

He wasted no time using the key and rushing into the office, where he found his Colt Navy and gun belt in a lower desk drawer. Slocum fastened the cross-draw holster around his waist, then sped to the door and peered outside. He had to get out of town fast without being seen.

Slocum pressed himself flat and closed the door to a mere crack when a solitary rider came up slowly, leading a second horse. In the darkness he couldn't see who it was. A soft voice called to him.

"Hurry, John. Yarrow'll be back in a few minutes. It won't take long for Mrs. McKean to get tired of him and shoo him away."

He slipped out, winced as the bell clanged loud enough to wake the dead, then climbed onto the horse Helen Murchison had brought for him.

"I don't know how to thank you."

"You didn't eat the key. That was a start."

"How'd you get it?" Slocum asked the dark-haired beauty. She was dressed in jeans and a man's plaid work shirt that did nothing to conceal her womanly charms. Helen had a big, floppy hat pulled down low on her forehead, but some of her luxurious hair spilled out, no matter how she tried to push it back to hide it.

"I took it off the key ring when he wasn't looking. The marshal isn't a very alert man, if you hadn't noticed." Helen laughed. "Enough talk. Let's ride. I know a place a few miles outside town where we can hole up for the night, but getting there's going to take a spot of hard riding."

She put spurs to her horse and rocketed off. Slocum followed, seeing that she took side streets and back alleys to keep from attracting too much attention. Before he knew it, they had left Moab far behind in its deep, cradling valley and worked their way up a switchback trail to the western rim of the canyon, looking down on the town.

Down on the valley floor lay Moab with its flickering gaslights and boisterous laughter boiling up from distant saloons, but Slocum had no idea where this trail led. That meant he had to do some scouting before he found his way back to where the stagecoach had been taken. That was his only chance for finding the gold and the men who had slaughtered Old Pete and the two passengers. Given Marshal Yarrow's limited mental capacity, Slocum doubted bringing the outlaws in would clear him, but he didn't care. There was another way to bring justice to the road agents.

Lead justice, the kind from the muzzle of his six-shooter.

"Ahead," Helen said. "There's a line shack where we can talk."

"I'm not much for talking," Slocum said.

"Good," Helen replied, smiling. "I don't feel much like talking right now, either."

She trotted ahead, letting him trail her. Slocum wondered what was going on. Helen Murchison was a lot more competent than she had any right being. Another mystery to be solved, but he didn't want to spend much time on it. He had a trail to follow and men to capture—or kill.

"I found this shack while riding around yesterday," she said, dismounting and tying her horse to a rail fastened onto a crude watering trough. Helen went into the cabin, leaving Slocum to tend the horses. Slocum's horse headed for the water and dunked its head in. He tied the reins around the same rail, took off the two horses' saddles and stowed them against a wall, covered them with a tarp he found to protect them against the harsh elements, then went into the shack. Helen already had a small fire built in the cast iron Franklin stove dominating the center of the room.

"Cozy," Slocum said, looking around. The room had been stripped bare, except for the stove and a pile of straw in one corner that served as a bed.

"I've slept in worse," Helen said.

"That surprises me," Slocum said. "You look like the kind of woman who only sleeps on feather beds in fine mansions."

"Do I now?" she said, laughing. Helen tossed off her hat, sending it spinning into the far corner of the room.

She ran her hands through the long, dark locks. Her bright blue eyes fixed on Slocum.

"Yeah," he said.

"You're right about one thing," Helen said, moving closer, until her breasts crushed into his chest. She tilted her head back slightly and closed her eyes. "I prefer the best in everything. Sometimes I don't get it."

"And sometimes you do," Slocum finished for her, bending down to kiss her fully on the lips. His heart hammered away as he tasted the sweetness there and felt her strong body pressing even more firmly against his. His arms circled her easily and held her close.

Their lips parted by mutual consent and tongues began dueling, stroking, slipping over one another and then playing hide-and-seek. Slocum slid his hands down Helen's back and found her buttocks, taut and round and malleable. He began kneading them like erotic lumps of dough. This caused Helen to widen her stance slightly, then lift one trim leg and hook it around his waist so she could rub her crotch up and down against him.

Slocum broke off the deep kiss and smiled. "Are you purring yet?"

"Because I'm stroking myself against you like a cat?" Helen kept her leg around him and leaned back a little. This forced out her breasts and gave Slocum a sight that caused his manhood to stir. Her breasts strained hard against the shirt she wore. Somehow, she managed to get the top two buttons unfastened without touching them. Slocum bent down and finished the job with his teeth, until her shirttail hung out and her chest was deliciously bare.

The twin mounds of her snowy white flesh drew Slocum's mouth like a lodestone inexorably attracts iron. He licked and kissed first one luscious hillock and then the other. He noted that Helen had stopped talking. She gasped in pleasure as he swooped down first on her left boob and then went to her right. Each time he caught the tiny red nubbin of flesh at the crest between his lips and suckled powerfully, then pushed it away with the tip of his tongue.

"I . . . I'm getting weak in the legs, John," Helen murmured. "Let's lie down. The straw is fresh."

Slocum reached down and again clutched at her perky behind. This time he lifted her easily and swung her around so he carried her in his arms. As they went to the pile of straw, he kissed her closed eyes and cheeks and forehead, then gently sank down and lavished more kisses on her bare breasts—and lower.

Helen struggled on the straw, moaning and writhing from side to side. Slocum worked around her waist and finally got his fingers under the waistband of her jeans to unfasten the button. It popped free, and he stripped off her tight-fitting pants as if he were peeling a banana.

"Yes, do it. I want to feel your mouth down there, John. I—oh!"

She gasped as he plunged downward, found the fleecy dark triangle and thrust his tongue out hard and fast. He entered her orally, roved about and then slid free to kiss the tender nether lips. The salty tang spurred him on. He left behind the tempting gateway into the sultry woman's fastness and kissed her inner thighs.

Her legs parted of their own accord. By now Slocum was beginning to feel some discomfort. He rocked back and quickly discarded his gun belt and freed his straining stalk of manhood from its cloth prison.

"So big," Helen said in a husky voice, looking down at him. "I knew it!"

Slocum bent over, hands on either side of the woman's trim body. His hips levered forward and he sank deep into her heated interior. Helen cried out and began thrashing about. Slocum drove himself even deeper into her core, relishing the heat and pressure all around his hidden length. For a delicious moment, Slocum did nothing but

savor the sensations ripping into his loins, then he began
to retreat. Slowly. Inch by inch.

The deliberate withdrawal pushed Helen's desires to an
even higher level. She reached up and clawed at his shoulders and hunched up to cram herself down around his
departing shaft.

"I want you, I want you so," she sobbed out.

He kept pulling back until only the thick head remained
hidden away inside her pink nether lips. Then Slocum
realized he shared her need for complete satisfaction.
There was nothing slow or easy about his reentry. The
force of the impact rocked them both. Helen's legs curled
up and locked around his hips to keep him from teasing
her as he had done before. But Slocum was past that.

He began moving with short, quick strokes intended to
push the beautiful woman quickly over the brink of ec-
stasy. The friction between his sliding iron pole and her
tightly clinging, excitement-moistened female sheath
burned away at his self-control. As if in the distance, over
the pounding in his ears, Slocum heard Helen cry out in
desire.

He kept pistoning back and forth, the carnal heat
mounting within his groin until he could no longer stand
it. A huge gout of burning lava spewed forth and set off
yet another reaction of pure hedonistic delight in the
woman. Slocum arched his back and tried to split her
apart with his fleshy lance. He brought forth another,
smaller shudder of rapturous release from her before he
sank down, sweating and tired from the sexual effort.

"It got mighty hot in here," Slocum said as Helen snuggled close to him, her head resting on his shoulder.

"I shouldn't have built such a big fire."

"I didn't mean the stove," he said.

"Neither did I," Helen replied. Then she started kissing
at his chest and working lower, until another fire raged
through both of their bodies.

5

Helen Murchison stirred, rolled over and pulled the blanket up over her bare white shoulder, against the chill in the cabin. Then her nose twitched a little and her bright azure eyes popped open, fixing immediately on Slocum.

"You're fixing breakfast," she accused.

"Guilty," Slocum said, turning a piece of bacon on the top of the stove griddle. He had fixed about all he had found, which wasn't much, but the empty feeling in his belly told him a good breakfast now was better than a string of small tidbits throughout the day that would only torment him.

"I'm so hungry I could eat a horse," Helen said, sitting up. The blanket fell away and a ray of sunlight angled through a crack in the wall to highlight her full, pert breasts. Slocum felt a twinge when he saw her bold nakedness, yet he could never call her wanton like a pretty waiter girl at some saloon or a Cyprian peddling her body in some bagnio. Everything about Helen spoke of sophistication and even breeding.

But that didn't affect the way she so saucily presented her bare body to him for his approval. And Slocum did approve.

"Oh, very well," Helen said in resignation, seeing he wasn't going to abandon the food for another roll in the hay with her. She eased into her shirt and fastened the buttons. Slocum watched as every inch of snowy white skin vanished behind the blue-and-black plaid flannel, until there was nothing more to be seen than her striking face and clothed figure.

"Eat hearty," Slocum said, passing a piece of bacon to her on the tip of his knife. She took it, then juggled the hot meat until it cooled enough to gnaw on.

"Hmm, good," she said. Slocum knew she was lying. It was old, moldy, and he hadn't cooked it enough to get rid of the spoiled taste.

Then he tried a piece of his own and nodded. It tasted surprisingly good, considering its pedigree.

"What do we do first?" Helen asked.

"We?" Slocum's eyebrows arched. "We split up. You go back to town, and I'll get on the trail of the road agents."

"I want to go with you, John. I broke you out of jail. I've got a stake in finding those . . . murderers," Helen finished somewhat lamely. Slocum wondered what she had intended to say before catching herself.

"What's your stake in finding them?" he asked bluntly.

"They ripped up my clothing," Helen said, obviously choosing her words more carefully now. "I won't permit that. And they killed three men. I could have been a fourth victim."

"There's a lot about the robbery I don't understand. I never saw outlaws take a stagecoach before. In spite of what the marshal says about the gold shipment onboard, there's something else to figure out."

"Perhaps they didn't have the horses to transport so much gold, and left it in the stage."

Slocum shook his head. He saw Helen did not believe that for one instant. She only spoke to distract him from pressing her on why she wanted to risk her life going after the owlhoots.

"They had six horses from the stage team, if they wanted to transport the gold. Sixteen thousand dollars is a lot of gold, but not that much for even one of those horses. With six horses, they could have moved a whale of a lot more than was on the stage."

"I'm going with you," she said firmly.

"I'll have to track them across mighty rough terrain. In case you hadn't noticed, a mile or two off the road is rocky wilderness. If they get south into the canyon lands where the Colorado River winds around, finding them will take a powerful lot of tracking. Dangerous tracking."

"I won't get in the way."

Slocum looked at her and then laughed.

"If you ride in front of me, you'll distract me. And if you ride behind, I'll spend my whole time looking around."

"Then I'll ride beside you."

"No." This time Slocum's tone brooked no challenge. He had a rough, perilous trail in front of him, and no matter how handy Helen was with a shotgun, no matter how clever she was in getting around a lawman like Yarrow, Slocum couldn't allow her to divert his attention for even a second. More than this, it was his fight and not hers. She had only been a passenger. He had his honor to uphold and his duty to perform.

"I owe you for getting me out of jail, but I can't take you with me," he said.

"This sounds personal," Helen said. "You can ride on, you know. You can have the Pacific Ocean lapping around your ankles in a week or two. So what if the marshal puts out a wanted poster on your head? Head north to Montana or cross the border into Mexico where a U.S. reward wouldn't matter."

"It's personal," Slocum said. "I was hired to guard the

gold, whether I knew it or not. The road agents stole it, so I have to get it back for Wells Fargo. Those passengers' lives were my responsibility. They're dead because I failed. The least I can do is bring their killers in or see that a few rounds of six-gun justice are bestowed on them."

"Yarrow would shoot first and ask questions later if you rode into town with prisoners," Helen said.

"All the more reason for you to get back to Moab and watch for me, to keep him and that mob he was whipping up into a frenzy from lynching me before I turn over the real desperadoes."

"You have a one-track mind, John," she said in admiration.

Slocum laughed ruefully, then added, "There's something else I want. I want to see the marshal's face when he realizes how wrong he was."

"It'd take Yarrow a month of Sundays before he came to believe you aren't guilty," Helen warned.

"Help me out by softening him up while I'm finding those owlhoots."

Helen heaved a deep sigh. Slocum enjoyed the rise and fall of her chest, and the way she brushed back the raven's-wing dark hair from her face. Then he pulled himself back to the chore in front of him. Let Helen use her wiles on the marshal. Slocum had to keep his ear to the ground to find where the outlaws had taken the stagecoach—and why.

"There's a cache of food out back," Helen said, as she came to what appeared to be a difficult conclusion for her. "I left it there when I found the cabin, just in case I needed a supply point."

Again Slocum marveled at how the woman's mind worked. At times she was more like an army general planning a major campaign than anything else. And then there were some very unmilitary points about her.

"I'll be back soon," he promised.

"I'll be waiting," Helen said. "Until then, let me give you a little reminder of *why* you ought to come back." She began unbuttoning the flannel shirt she had so carefully fastened earlier. Slocum wasn't going to argue with her this time.

Slocum rode more on instinct than skill from tracking. The rocky ground afforded no hint of the stagecoach or its recent passage. He had gone to the spot where he had last seen the stage and then had taken the narrow canyon trail denied him before. Slocum kept a sharp eye out for Yarrow and his posse, but the lawman had retreated to Moab and wasn't venturing beyond the city limits to hunt for the real culprits.

That suited Slocum just fine. It kept him from having to look over his shoulder all the time waiting for the marshal to bungle onto his back trail. By noon Slocum was lost in the fairyland of wind-eroded arches and bright red- and yellow- and gray-streaked rock. He hardly noticed the formations like upright decks of stony cards, or the caves bored into the rocky faces, because he had found fresh scat from several horses along the trail.

Slocum ate a cold lunch as he rode, not wanting to take the time to dismount and fix a decent meal. He was glad he had eaten well that morning because he felt time closing in him like the jaws of a vise. The longer he took to find the outlaws' trail, the more likely they were to be out of the territory entirely.

Still, Slocum wondered at the signs he found. No stagecoach tracks, no hoofprints, only fresh horse manure from a dozen ponies. When he found another warm pile drawing flies, Slocum slid from the saddle, found a short stick and poked through the heap. He frowned. The horse depositing this had eaten prickly pear pads and little else.

That was an unusual meal to feed a horse—for a white man.

He rocked back on his heels, then jumped to his feet when a single rifle shot echoed down the canyon and rolled past him. Slocum grabbed the reins and led his horse down into a sandy-bottomed arroyo, where he tied it up so he could advance on foot to see who was doing some twilight hunting.

As careful as Slocum was, he almost stumbled over a young Crow brave hunkered down behind a large greasewood bush, waiting for a rabbit to poke its head out of a burrow. As still as death, the Indian held a bow with an arrow nocked, waiting patiently. Slocum held his breath. The bow and arrow told Slocum there was at least one other hunter with a rifle—the one who had fired.

His hand flashed to the Colt Navy at his hip when the Crow boiled from his hiding place, but Slocum relaxed when he saw that the Indian's attention was entirely on a scrawny cottontail. With unerring accuracy, the Crow loosed his arrow and caught the rabbit behind the shoulder. The rabbit's lungs collapsed and it let out a shrill screech caused by air rushing out the hole before it died.

Slocum silently followed the brave back to camp and watched as the young buck proudly held up his kill. Two other hunters worked to skin their kill, and a third rabbit had already been spitted, waiting only for the cooking fire to be lit.

Keeping flat on his belly, Slocum waited a half hour before he was sure the six Crow were the only ones in this hunting party. But something struck him as wrong. They went after deer, not rabbits, if they were hunting for the tribe. That meant they were on some other mission and sought only filler for their own taut bellies.

The cooking odor drifting in Slocum's direction made his mouth water, but he wasn't going to leave until he figured out what the Indians were up to. The six finished their meal, laughing and joking. Slocum wasn't well enough versed in the Crow tongue to make out what they were saying, but he thought one wanted to race another with a heavy bet on the outcome. To his surprise, the rest of the Crow denied him his race. This alone would have been enough to alert Slocum that something odd was in the wind. The Crow were great gamblers and never passed on the chance to lay a wager, especially on a horse race.

But they did now.

Slocum took note then of other details he had missed. The Indians weren't pitching camp for the night. They had stopped for dinner but were now moving on in the dark. When he realized this, Slocum edged away silently, then hurried back to where he had tethered his horse. The mare had found a few juicy leaves from low bushes and looked content now that it had rested. Still, the animal protested when Slocum climbed back into the saddle.

"We can rest soon," Slocum said, patting the horse on the neck. The horse seemed to understand and resigned itself to more travel that night.

Slocum cocked his head to one side and listened hard, then smiled. He had been right. The sound of the Crow ponies traveling over rock assured him they were on the trail again. Slocum followed at a distance, not sure why he bothered with them since they weren't responsible for the stagecoach robbery. Some instinct told him he would learn something important if he kept in the shadows and just observed.

A few miles later, the canyon opened onto a broad vista. In the distance Slocum heard the gurgling of a fast-running river. He wasn't sure where he was but thought the Indians were heading toward the Colorado River. They might want to water their horses after a dry trip through the rock and sand of the rugged Utah desert, but he didn't think so. They were too intent on reaching some specific point.

The rendezvous became apparent when Slocum reached the top of a hill sloping straight down to the riverbank. Already there, three men sat near a roaring campfire. The trio stood and waved in greeting as the Crow approached. They didn't appear uneasy at the notion of being outnumbered and having Indians ride up on them in the dark.

Slocum tugged on the reins and circled, coming up on the gathering from upstream. The rush of water hid any small sound he or his horse might make as he sneaked up on the camp. He was immediately glad he was in no hurry to get closer when he saw part of the reason that the three men in the camp weren't upset over being outnumbered by the Crow. He found a man with a rifle hidden some distance from camp, watching intently for any treachery on the Indians' part.

Slocum dismounted and went closer on foot, avoiding the armed sentry. The dark and the constant noise from the river racing wildly down its streambed let him get close enough to hear what the men in camp were saying.

". . . glad you could make it tonight, Blue Claw. Have some coffee," offered the man Slocum pegged as the leader of those in the camp. The other two stood with their backs to Slocum.

The Crow chief stepped forward and took the tin cup in both hands, glanced at the white man, then drank down the coffee. He coughed once, spat, then nodded.

"Good," Blue Claw declared.

"Not anywhere near as good as what we got to offer you." The man motioned and the other two jumped to action, pulling back a tarp and revealing a long wooden box.

Slocum caught his breath. He recognized the case as one holding Army rifles. Spencers. He had blundered onto a gunrunner selling Indians illicit arms.

Then he realized he had found more than this. One of the men struggling with the rope handle to move the case closer to the fire turned his face in Slocum's direction. Slocum forced himself to remain calm and not draw down on the man—this was the man he had seen most clearly driving the stolen stagecoach. Slocum had found the road agents. They also happened to be gunrunners.

"Only one case? We want more. Many more," Blue Claw declared.

"We can get you as many as you like. Ten cases? A hundred."

"One hundred cases?" The Indian frowned. Slocum saw him struggle with the numbers. "Two thousand rifles?"

"Not a problem," the gunrunner said, smiling. Slocum knew lies went along with such illegal activity, but he had the ugly feeling the man wasn't lying. If Blue Claw wanted two thousand rifles, they were his—for a price.

"You sell rifles but not the ammunition," Blue Claw said truculently. "We no use rifles for clubs. Have clubs, need rifles and ammunition."

"It's easy to see that you haven't dealt with me before, Chief. I supply what you need. There's no reason for me to cheat you. Five hundred rounds for each rifle sound good to you?"

"Even if I buy two thousand rifles?"

Slocum thought the Indian chief was joking. The gunrunner didn't take it that way.

"I want to be straight with you about this. Can't lay my hands on that much ammo. I can only furnish three hundred rounds, but that ought to do you, even if you want to wage war on the entire territory."

"How much?" asked Blue Claw.

"I can give you a break on the price if you really want a hundred cases of rifles."

"Ten," Blue Claw said. "Ten cases. Ten thousand rounds of ammo."

They got down to dickering, the specifics mostly lost in the noise from the river. Slocum lay flat on his belly, studying the details of the gunrunners' camp for some clue to the location of the gold. They wouldn't be foolish enough to bring it to a meeting with a Crow war party. Slocum watched the one outlaw he recognized, then studied the two with him, especially the one who acted as leader. When the Crow left after smoking a pipe to close the deal, Slocum intended to follow the gunrunners and get to the bottom of their vile business dealings. Somehow, it involved highway robbery.

The end of the discussion came suddenly. Blue Claw made a chopping motion with his hand, as if he were cutting off the gunrunner's head. The Crow party mounted and rode off without their traditional pipe smoking, leaving the three men in camp smiling.

Slocum caught a wisp of conversation.

"They'll pay the price," the leader said. "These are brand spankin' new rifles and nobody else'd sell to the Crow."

"Mighty steep price, though, Ray," said the one Slocum recognized.

"They'll pay. Let's get the hell out of here."

Slocum's heart raced. They were returning to their camp—where the stolen gold might be stashed. He didn't have to tangle with the Crow now. He had started to get to his feet when he heard heavy footsteps behind him crunching through dried vegetation.

A rifle cocked and an angry voice called, "Who's there?"

6

Slocum froze. His hand rested on the ebony handle of his six-shooter but he didn't draw. Any movement would give him away now.

"Come on out!" shouted the sentry. "I got you in my sights, you mangy varmint!"

Slocum wasn't sure if he or the man with the rifle was the most startled when a small coyote burst from the protection of a low-growing creosote bush and bolted for the river, a brown smear melting quickly into the night. The gunrunner jerked his rifle up and fired wildly at the spooked predator.

"What's going on out there?" called the leader.

"I flushed a coyote, Ray. Nuthin' more'n that," the sentry said.

"Well, quit wastin' bullets and get your ass back here right now. We got to move out."

Slocum remained as frozen as a fawn when the gunrunner passed within five feet without spotting him. He sank down, ready for action if any in the camp saw him, but they were intent on selling rifles to the Indians and gathered around the fire for a quick council. From other directions came two more sentries. If the Crow had tried to steal the single crate of rifles, they would have found themselves on the receiving end of a powerful load of lead from the hidden snipers.

As it was, Slocum knew better than to tangle with the outlaws. One of them had been part of the stagecoach robbery, and he suspected the rest were involved, too. They were cold-blooded murderers and would certainly kill again if anyone tried to nix their sale of rifles to the Crow. The Indians might be planning a major war and need the rifles to fight the Army, or the small band Slocum had seen might constitute the full uprising. Either way, the Crow had money the gunrunners wanted.

But if these gunrunners were also the stage robbers, the gold they had stolen must not be enough for them. Slocum knew that greedy men were doubly dangerous—and doubly vulnerable. All he had to do was wait for them to overstep.

He reached his horse, climbed into the saddle and then checked that the rifle in the saddle sheath was loaded and ready for action. The Winchester's magazine held four rounds. Slocum looked in the saddlebags for more ammo and found nothing. He had the provisions Helen had provided but not enough ammo to fight a protracted gunfight. That meant he had to be even cagier when he found the gold and captured the road agents.

Slocum heard the men down by the river, then saw the faint flicker from their campfire vanish. A few minutes later, horses' hooves clattered on the rock and finally disappeared. The gunrunners rode down to the sandy shoreline of the river, heading deeper into the twisting labyrinth of canyons to the south. Slocum set out after them, hoping to keep a decent distance back so they wouldn't spot him. Not keeping them in sight quickly worked against him.

He came to a forking canyon where a smaller stream fed into the raging Colorado. In the dark, he couldn't tell if the gunrunners had continued along the river or had gone up the narrow canyon cut by the tributary. Fuming at the time it would take but seeing no way around it, Slocum dismounted, dropped to his hands and knees and began carefully studying the ground.

The tracks he found were muddled, as if several mounted riders had waited here on nervously prancing horses. Slocum ran his finger along the ridge fashioned in the sand by a single hoofprint. He didn't like risking it but saw no way around exposing his position. Slocum had to find out where the gunrunners had ridden. Taking out a lucifer, he struck it on sandpaper glued to the lid of the tin box and held the flame down close to the ground.

"Damn," he muttered. These tracks weren't from shod horses.

Hastily snuffing out the sulfurous match, Slocum got to his feet in time to see a dark shadow flitting ahead of him. He swung around and saw several more cutting him off from the canyon where the Colorado flowed so swiftly. He was caught between two bands of the Crow.

Slocum considered bluffing his way out of the trap by telling Blue Claw he was one of Ray's men and wanted to renegotiate the gun deal. Somehow, he doubted that would work. If anything, Blue Claw would see him as a bargaining chip or simply kill him out of spite because Ray had insisted on getting top dollar for the rifles. Even if he had been one of the gunrunners, Slocum doubted Ray would be willing to give up even a dime in ransom, no matter how much the Crow chief threatened.

For anyone else, the gunrunner would have even less sympathy.

And if Ray or the outlaw who had been driving the stagecoach recognized Slocum, hell would be out for lunch. They would gladly let the Crow do what they wanted with their captive. Slocum had heard stories from old mountain men about what the Crow could do and wanted to avoid finding out firsthand if any of those tales were true.

Slocum grabbed the reins of his horse and vaulted into the saddle. The mare protested a mite, then settled down. Slocum would have to thank Helen for giving him such a fine horse; he couldn't have picked one with a stouter heart himself. Keeping low, hugging the horse's neck, Slocum slowly walked the mare away from the Colorado, finding a smaller tributary pouring from another canyon. He had no other escape. Slocum rode into the canyon, trying to avoid the stream because letting his horse walk in it would slow him considerably. Better to stick to solid ground.

He wasn't fooling the Indians, but if he didn't present a silhouette for them to shoot at they might think the horse was a stray and come for it. That could give him a moment of surprise to use to his advantage. But the Crow weren't likely to let a stray horse wander off on its own. Horses meant wealth to the Indians. A horse without an owner was the same as finding a twenty-dollar gold piece in the dust.

"Come on," Slocum quietly urged, getting the horse moving a bit faster. He headed for the nearer canyon wall. Finding a path to the rim was out of the question. Even if it had been broad daylight, hitting upon and following such a narrow ledge of rock was dangerous. With a band of Indians behind him, it was suicidal.

He reached the rocky face and started back toward the Colorado, only to hear the Crow talking among themselves. At least four blocked his path. Slocum sawed at the reins and got the horse headed in the other direction, up the canyon and away from the gunrunners. He cursed his bad luck, but every second he kept his scalp now meant another second to escape.

He hadn't ridden a hundred yards when he came on a Crow standing with a rifle resting in the crook of his left arm. The sentry came forward, then let out a whoop of glee. In the dark he didn't see that Slocum clung to the horse; he thought he had found a stray pony.

Slocum hung on the left side of the horse while the brave came up on the right. In a dangerous move, Slocum let himself slide all the way around and beneath the horse's belly. The move spooked the horse and alerted the warrior, but Slocum reached out and grabbed an ankle and yanked as hard as he could. The Crow's moccasined foot sailed from under him. Flailing wildly, he toppled back and banged his head hard against a rock.

Slocum landed on the ground and covered his head with his arms to keep his prancing horse from kicking him. He rolled away and came to his knees, knife in hand and ready to slit the fallen brave's throat. There was no need. The man's head lay at a crazy angle. He had broken his neck in the fall.

Grabbing the dead warrior's rifle gave Slocum a few more rounds he could put to good use in a fight. Nothing else at the brave's belt interested him, except two fresh scalps. The Crow were definitely on the warpath.

Slocum took his horse's reins again and walked quickly away from the slowly cooling corpse. If he had even a ghost of a chance before, it had vanished with the death of the brave. The Crow would want vengeance on anyone killing one of their own. Slocum blundered along, got tangled up in dense undergrowth and then backtracked to get around it. As he found a decent trail leading deeper into the canyon, he heard a loud cry of rage. The dead Crow warrior had been discovered.

Slocum threw caution to the winds, mounted and gave the horse its head. He had to trust the horse's instincts not to step into a rabbit burrow or snake hole in the dark. If the horse broke its leg, he was a goner. Even if it didn't, Slocum knew from the ruckus behind him that he would be in for a big fight. The Crow let out war whoops in his direction and shouted what could only be insults.

He rode even faster, desperately looking for a way out of the canyon. Every dark recess set his heart racing as he thought he had found a branching canyon. As quickly as hope rose, it was dashed. Crevices abounded—but none afforded him a way out. The Crow had him effectively bottled up unless the far end provided some much needed relief.

It didn't. Slocum went cold all over when he saw he had ridden into a box canyon divided into two neat sections by a powerfully flowing stream. In the bright Utah daylight he might have found a path to the rim amid the sandy, crumbling red rock, but in the dark that was out of the question. Even worse, he rode through a sandy spit where a cooking fire showed the remains of a roasted wild turkey. His horse's hooves kicked up the discarded feathers as Slocum looked around desperately. He had found the Crow campsite when he had wanted to avoid it.

He rode to the water's edge and splashed along the stream to the end of the canyon, where a waterfall cascaded down fifty feet from above. Any hope of finding a way out disappeared entirely.

Fight or hide were his only chances since flight was out of the question.

"Come on," Slocum said, getting his horse to splash through the river. He rode directly under the waterfall and found a small cave behind the frothy curtain. Slocum dismounted and took the brave's rifle, knelt and trained the sights on a spot near the Crow camp where the Indians were most likely to appear.

One showed up, pointing to the tracks he had left. Slocum had started to shoot the brave when two more came up. They were joined by six more. Slocum sagged a mite in despair. He couldn't tell which was Blue Claw, and it hardly mattered. He could kill their chief but the rest would end his life fast. All it would take was one concentrated charge.

Slocum moved the sights from one Indian to the next, vainly trying to pick out their chief. He hadn't gotten that good a look at Blue Claw, and the Crow were decked out in similar war paint. All that kept him from firing methodically into the tight knot back at their campsite was the way they milled around in confusion.

Hope began to mount that he had thrown them off his trail by going into the water. How long that tactic would work depended on how angry the braves were at him for killing their sentry.

Slocum lifted the rifle and took aim when he figured out which of the Crow was Blue Claw. The one strutting around, shouting orders and pointing up at the canyon rims had to be their leader. But Slocum couldn't figure what Blue Claw was saying or looking at.

From behind the curtain of falling water, he couldn't see anything more than the campsite.

The Crow began looking in the direction their leader pointed and soon drifted away, then mounted their horses. Slocum tensed when Blue Claw stared directly at him. He was sure the Crow chief's vision penetrated the cascading water. Even after Blue Claw spun about, mounted his horse and rode away, Slocum didn't relax.

He was drenched, cold and miserable, but he wasn't going to stir from the hidey-hole until he was sure he wasn't going to draw attention to himself. If the Crow had an inkling he was crouching behind the waterfall, they would have come for him.

An hour later Slocum ventured out to see what had drawn the Crow away. He stared up at the canyon rim but saw nothing until, from the corner of his eye, he caught movement. Slocum spun and stared directly at a light bobbing about along the far rim. Whoever was up there had drawn away Blue Claw and his warriors. Whether they thought Slocum had grown wings and flown up there or simply wanted to see who held the high ground, he didn't know.

It didn't matter.

He led his horse from behind the waterfall and mounted. The saddle was soaked and the horse was miserable.

"We'll both be a lot worse off if we don't get out of here fast," he told the horse. The mare understood what it meant to be taken as a Crow pony; it set off at a brisk walk.

Every nerve in Slocum's body twitched at the slightest noise in the night. He thought Blue Claw and the rest of the Crow band had taken a hidden path to the top of the canyon, but he couldn't be sure they hadn't left one or two behind as guards on the rocky floor. They used this canyon as a camp and wouldn't want the cavalry riding in and catching them unawares.

Slocum cut away from the middle of the canyon where the stream flowed and retraced his path along the canyon wall. When he reached the spot where the brave had died, he looked around and saw faint dark shapes moving along the rim, occasionally blocking the brighter stars to confirm their existence.

Blue Claw had gone off on a wild-goose chase. Or at least the Crow had lit out after whoever carried the lantern.

Slocum heaved a sigh of relief when he reached the mouth of the canyon where the tributary flowed into the Colorado. He had escaped the Crow. Now he had to find the gunrunners.

7

Slocum wobbled in the saddle by the time the sun poked its fiery edge above the canyon rim. He had ridden all night, wary of Crow on his trail and constantly worried that he might stumble across the gunrunners' camp unexpectedly in the dark. Neither Indian nor outlaw had shown so much as a hair. When his mare stumbled several times in a few minutes, as determined as he was, Slocum knew he had to take a rest.

He dismounted and let the weary horse drink its fill from the Colorado, then led it into the sagebrush some distance away, where it could graze on a thick patch of gray-green buffalo grass. Preparing himself a cold meal, he ate without tasting the food. He swallowed mechanically, his mind on nothing but his search for the gunrunners.

Slocum was positive they were also the road agents who had robbed the Wells Fargo stage and had killed Old Pete along with the two passengers. Bringing the gang down would remove a powerful lot of crime from the territory and might earn him a reward from Wells Fargo as well as the Army. All Slocum had to do was avoid Marshal Yarrow long enough to explain how he had come to bring in the robbers.

Slocum shook his head to clear out the fuzziness. He was jumping the gun by a considerable margin. Before he brought them in along with the gold, he had to catch them and find what they had done with the gold shipment. Capturing six murderers wasn't going to be easy. Finding the gold might be even harder.

"Hell," he muttered to himself, "didn't I get away from a Crow war party intent on lifting my scalp?" When Slocum realized what he had said aloud, he knew he needed sleep badly. He had shown minimal skill escaping the Crow, and he knew better than to rely too much on luck.

Lady Luck had a tendency to look the other way when he needed her most. Better to use his quick wits and quicker six-gun.

Slocum curled up in his blanket, fell asleep immediately, then began tossing and turning as the heat began filling the canyon like a rain barrel about ready to burst. When the sweltering temperature became too much to sleep through even in his exhausted condition, Slocum gave in to necessity. He checked his watch, saw he had snatched about four hours of sleep, then got his horse ready for the trail again.

The short nap had taken the edge off his fatigue, but he knew he wasn't sharp enough to take on Ray and his outlaw gang. All day Slocum dozed in the saddle, but he finally snapped awake when the air turned from blast-furnace hot to downright chilly. The sun had sunk, and the surrounding rock quickly surrendered its heat back to the sky. The bracing cold brought him completely awake—or was it the sound of a horse clumping along the canyon?

Slocum reined in and waited, every sense alert. The canyon spread out for almost a half mile, the Colorado River running smack down the middle, making a constant clashing din. For the sound of a horse to be so obvious, the rider had to be nearby. Slocum caught sight of the rider on the far side of the river, chin down on chest and probably grabbing some shut-eye, giving his horse its head as if it knew where its owner intended to go.

The twilight deepened, giving Slocum even more cover as he forded the river and trailed the lone rider. This might be a cowpoke on his way out of the canyon lands to find work on a spread. Or it could be an honest pilgrim choosing to come this way because it was easier than going around the vast array of canyons cut into the heart of the world by the energetic Colorado River.

Still, in spite of other possibilities, Slocum figured the rider probably had business with the gunrunners. With the Crow kicking up such a fuss, the whole area had to be too dangerous for anyone not in a powerful hurry. From the look of the rider bouncing along, half-asleep, he wasn't in any hurry at all.

"Who's there?" came the sharp challenge.

The rider Slocum trailed jerked upright in the saddle even as Slocum dropped to the ground and yanked at his horse's reins to get out of sight. In the darkness he hadn't spotted the guard.

"You know who it is," the man said querulously. "It's me. Hugh Welkin. I got business with Ray."

"You alone?" asked the guard.

"You blind as a bat? Look around. Does it look like I'm leading a parade of elephants? Of course I'm alone. That's the only way I deal."

"Sorry," the guard said, not too contritely. "Camp's a quarter mile downriver, up against the canyon wall."

Welkin grumbled to himself as he put the spurs to his horse, rocketing off. Slocum moved closer and saw the sentry make an obscene gesture and mutter about how high-and-mighty Welkin thought he was. The guard rested his rifle against a rock, sat next to it and began building himself a cigarette from fixings stashed in his pocket.

While the man worked, Slocum slipped past and advanced on foot. His feet began hurting by the time he reached a spot amid damp rocks where spray from the river caused a constant rain. But he saw Welkin and the outlaw leader near a fire and found it easier to ignore his own discomfort. Slocum felt like he was reaching the end of the trail—or at least was closer to figuring out who the players in this gunrunning drama were.

He looked up and saw two outlaws perched in shallow caves on the cliff face next to the camp. Ray always guarded his back with snipers, but Slocum had seen first-hand that they weren't too alert. Or maybe they were more interested in what Welkin had to say. The words coming through the river's roar certainly interested Slocum.

"I can get you all the rifles you want," Hugh Welkin boasted, puffing out his chest and putting his thumbs in his armpits as if he were the cock of the walk.

"We want more'n rifles," Ray said.

"The ammunition," Welkin said, nodding in agreement. "Rifles ain't no good without something to put in them."

"You have any Gatling guns?"

For a moment Slocum thought Welkin was going to swallow his own tongue. He turned red in the face and sputtered a little before he answered.

"I can't get anything like that."

"How about a mountain howitzer or two?"

"That would cost you dearly," Welkin said. "I can get the rifles—and a mountain howitzer."

"With the gunpowder and shot for it?" Ray refilled his coffee cup from a pot sitting in the fire. He didn't offer any to his visitor.

"You can use links of chain. Why steal cannonballs?" Welkin rubbed his hands against his trousers. "Getting it will be real expensive. A thousand dollars."

"Two howitzers with all the paraphernalia, twenty cases of Spencers and ammo—sure you can't get a Gatling?— and maybe an officer's saber."

"What do you want a saber for?" asked Welkin, startled at the request.

"Trade goods. I can get anything I want from my, uh, customers, by trading them a sword."

"You're sellin' to the Crow, ain't you? Wait, never mind. That's not my business. You pony up the gold and I'll get you all the rifles you want."

"What we've ordered," Ray said. "How much?"

Welkin turned cagey as he said, "Twenty thousand. In gold. None of that worthless scrip the Mormons issue in their banks."

"Ten thousand in bullion," countered Ray.

The dickering went on until Hugh Welkin agreed to $15,000 in gold.

"I'll tell you where we swap the gold for the guns," Welkin said. "You know how I work. You'll have to provide your own wagons. That's part of the deal."

"You keep harping on that. Don't worry. I got myself a jim-dandy way of transportin' the weapons. Even the cannon."

"How's that?" asked Welkin.

"Let's just say I can deliver the mail along with the rifles to the Crow," Ray said, laughing. Welkin looked confused but Slocum now understood the reason for taking the stagecoach. It made for a fine wagon to move a dozen crates of rifles and even a howitzer or two. Welkin had to be stealing the rifles from an Army post; the cavalry would be on the lookout for a wagon transporting the illicit arms but might ignore a Wells Fargo Concord coach.

"We got a deal. Next week. You know the place."

"Midnight on the tenth," Ray agreed. He tossed out the dregs of his coffee and stood.

Welkin reached out to shake hands but Ray ignored the gesture. Welkin let his hand drop to his side, where he rubbed his palm dry again. No matter how confident he sounded, Slocum knew the man had to be as nervous as a virgin whore at a Green River rendezvous from the way he acted. Ray and his gang were tough customers, and any misstep would mean lead flying.

"Don't worry your head none, Ray," Welkin said. "I've done this before. The Army supply officer's so dumb he still doesn't know what happened to the last couple crates of rifles."

"Stealing two cases of rifles is a damned sight easier than making off with what we're talking about," Ray said.

"The gold's a big incentive," Welkin declared too loudly. "You get it ready and I'll see you next week." He started to offer his handshake again to cement the deal and saw Ray wasn't inclined now either. Somewhat awkwardly, Hugh Welkin went to his horse and rode from the outlaw camp.

Ray sat for a few minutes, then waved to the riflemen in the rocks above him. They made their way to sit and sampled some of the coffee.

"Everything ready to go, Boss?" asked the outlaw Slocum recognized from the stage robbery.

"Everything's fine as frog's fur," Ray said. He worked his jaw around and ground his teeth. "I worry about old Hugh, though. That boy's greedy and stupid. A bad combination."

"We can ride on out with the gold we already got. There's plenty to go around," spoke up another road agent.

"We've been over that, Slim," Ray said harshly. "We can ride out of Utah with three times as much, thanks to the Crow. They're intendin' to start one hell of a war and are willing to pay for their rifles."

"Almost fifty thousand dollars," mused Slim. "That's a real incentive."

"Not a bad return on sixteen thousand dollars," Ray said.

Slocum pricked up his ears. Ray was going to keep some of the gold for himself. The deal he had wrangled with Welkin was for only $15,000.

"Even if we don't get near that much from Blue Claw, we'll still see a passel more than we got now. We know he robbed two gold trains up north and hurrahed the bank at Price. No telling how many settlers he's scalped along the way. All we got to do is wait a week or so."

Slim seemed content with this.

"We can't sit on our butts," Ray declared. "We have to be ready. Don't think Welkin wouldn't double-cross us if he could, and you know Blue Claw would prefer to see our scalps dangling from his belt. We have to fetch the gold, get it moved to the place where we'll swap and then prepare to get the guns to the Crow."

"You know, Ray," spoke the outlaw Slocum had recognized, "we can take the guns from Welkin and never pay him a plugged nickel. He don't seem too smart to me."

"We need him to be the scapegoat for the cavalry, Marley. Otherwise, those bluecoats will be swarming all over us. By the time they figure Welkin's sold the guns, we'll have swapped them to the Crow and be on our way out of the territory."

"Sort of like a doorstop," Marley mused.

"How's that?" asked Ray, looking sharply at the outlaw.

"We toss him out and he keeps the door from openin' far enough for the cavalry to see us."

They finished their coffee, then kicked sand onto the fire. The area was plunged into darkness. Slocum settled down among the rocks and let his eyes adjust to the night while the outlaws broke camp. They were on their way to dig up the gold from wherever they had hidden it.

From the way Ray talked, it might be stored in the stagecoach. If so, that meant they had to leave the deep canyon and get to one rim or the other to head back in the direction of Moab. There was no way they could have brought a Concord coach down to the river bottom.

As Ray and Marley argued over shooting Hugh Welkin and stealing the rifles from him, Slocum slipped back along the path he had already taken. He could follow them, get the drop on the outlaws and be done with his dangerous chore.

In his hurry to get back to his horse, Slocum forgot about the lone sentry the outlaws had stationed along this trail. Slocum was swinging into the saddle when a cold voice ordered, "Get back down or I'll ventilate your worthless hide."

Slocum fumed at being so careless. He put it off to not getting enough sleep, but the reason hardly mattered.

"Howdy," he called, finding the dim shape against a patch of bushes. Slocum judged distances and his chance for unlimbering his six-shooter before the outlaw drilled him. He decided they weren't good. Faint starlight caught the front bead on the rifle and showed the muzzle pointed directly at him.

"Why're you spyin' on us?"

"I don't know what you mean," Slocum said. "I was just traveling along and had to answer a call to nature."

"Bullshit," the guard snarled. Slocum heard boots grinding against gravel as the man steadied his stance. "You was spyin' on us. Get down from that horse, or I swear I'll shoot you where you sit."

Slocum dropped back to the ground, waiting for an opening. Any opening. His heart turned into a cold knot when he saw that the outlaw was too wary.

"Good," the road agent said, approving of the way Slocum moved away from his horse. "There ain't no reason for you to be pokin' around unless you're after us for the reward."

Slocum's hand flashed for his six-gun, but he could never draw and fire accurately when his target was cloaked in shadow and already had the drop on him.

The rifle report echoed down the broad canyon.

8

Slocum stood stock-still, wondering if this was what it was like to be dead. It didn't feel different from being alive. His hand still rested on the butt of his six-shooter, the river still tumbled along fiercely a dozen yards away, flies buzzed around his head and the smell of sage and other growing things lingered in his nostrils.

He slid his six-gun from his holster and went to check the fallen outlaw. The man lay slumped on the sandy ground. Slocum rolled him over using the toe of his boot. Slocum's stomach turned; he had seen wounds this bad during the war, but not often. The man's face was an unrecognizable bloody mess. Closer examination showed a bullet had entered the back of the road agent's head, expanded to destroy his brain and finally blasted out through the face.

"A hell of a way to die," came a soft voice.

Slocum looked up.

"You saved my life." Slocum looked from the rifle held firmly in Helen Murchison's hands to her face. She was as lovely as ever but showed only a slight distaste for what she had just done. "He's dead."

"Good," Helen said with some rancor. "He deserved it."

"For trying to gun me down?"

"Quiet!" Helen stepped closer and tipped her head. She held up one hand to stifle any protest on his part. Slocum picked out the sounds from the night's background about the same time she did.

"It's the owlhoots who robbed the stage," Slocum said. "They heard the shot and are coming to find out what's going on." This time there wasn't a living outlaw to tell them he had flushed a coyote and fired wildly at it in the dark.

"Get your horse and let's ride," Helen said. Her attitude turned darker now, her jaw set and her face a mask of anger. She wasn't in any mood to argue, and Slocum wasn't inclined to shoot it out alone with Ray and the rest of his gang. Any element of surprise was long past, and with the killers alerted, the fight wasn't one he and Helen could win.

Slocum knew the gunshot had to have echoed for a ways, in spite of the noisy river. Ray would investigate even if he had been a mile down the river canyon.

Too much rode on the road agents' activities being kept under wraps for Ray to ignore even a small disturbance.

"You have a place to hide or do we just head on back to Moab at a gallop?" Slocum asked, riding shoulder to shoulder with Helen.

"They won't chase us too long. They don't know how many of us there are."

"Ray was going to get the gold he stole," Slocum said. "They might want to be sure it stays hidden until they find who killed their partner."

"Ray? You used to calling Ray Sanders by his first name?" Helen glared at him. Her face had softened a mite but not much. Whatever drove her was fueled by incredible anger.

"Never heard him called by his full name while I was spying on him and his gang," Slocum said. Such picayune details hardly mattered. Men put on and took off names at a whim out West. Nobody much cared and nobody asked without inviting a bellyful of lead as an answer.

"Ray Sanders," the dark-haired woman said positively. "As nasty a varmint as you'd ever want to cross. It figures he's the one involved in . . . all this." Helen finished her tirade a bit vaguely, as if she wanted to keep from telling Slocum too much.

"You a bounty hunter after him?" Slocum asked. "You surely do use that rifle well. And back in Moab, there wasn't any question how good you were with the shotgun. It was as if you'd been born with it in your hands."

"There," Helen said, pointing toward the shadowy cliff face. "I see a spot where we can hide. Sanders isn't likely to track us in the dark if we stay on the rocky patches while we get over there." She followed her own advice, slowing and letting her horse pick its way across a stretch of rock worn smooth by endless years of river flowing at spring highs. Slocum followed, occasionally glancing over his shoulder at their back trail. If the road agents hunted them, they were being mighty quiet about it.

Helen Murchison dismounted and led her horse into a narrow crevice, then vanished. For a moment Slocum hesitated; then he went after her. The break in the rock did not go directly into the cliff but broke off and turned at a right angle. Unless the outlaws were directly in the crevice mouth, they would never see Helen and Slocum taking refuge here.

"Nice spot to while away an hour or two," Slocum observed. "Or do you reckon they'll keep after us that long?"

"They're greedy sons of bitches," Helen said with rancor. "When they don't spot us right off, they'll go back to their camp to figure out what to do next."

"Ray—Sanders—was on his way to dig up the gold."

"Are you sure?" Helen spoke sharply and her blue eyes speared into him. He felt like a witness on the stand being interrogated.

"I kept my eyes and ears open." He hesitated to say much more.

"Did you see anyone else?"

"There was the owlhoot who drove the stage after they stole it. A man named Marley. And earlier I came across a band of Crow," he told her, suspecting that she actually asked after Hugh Welkin. For some reason, he held back telling her what she wanted to know. Helen had pulled his fat out of the fire twice. He might eventually have gotten away from Marshal Yarrow and the Moab jail, but the sentry had caught him flat-footed. Without her accurate, deadly shot, Slocum knew he would be the one drawing flies back by the riverside.

"I know what the Indians want," she said bitterly. "Who else have you seen? A stocky man, about your height or a little less, shifty eyes? Have you seen him?"

"Hugh Welkin?" Slocum asked, watching her closely for reaction. If he had stuck her with a pin, her response couldn't have been more pronounced.

"You *saw* him? What'd he have to say?"

"He's running guns. Sanders and his boys are using the gold from the robbery to buy rifles and a couple mountain howitzers. I'd say Welkin has a key to some Army arsenal."

"Howitzers?" Helen grumbled under her breath. "Which way'd he go?"

"Welkin can't be more than an hour or so off," Slocum said, trying to guess how much time had passed since the man had left Sanders's camp. "He rode back upriver, in the direction you came."

"I crossed the Colorado from the other side," Helen said.

"Were you on the far rim last night?" Slocum asked,

remembering the light that had distracted the Crow. "If that was you, I owe you my life another time."

"I have to catch him," Helen said.

"I want the gold. I owe it to Gus Riordan to recover the gold for the company."

"Wells Fargo will never miss it," Helen said, distracted. "Help me catch Welkin, and I'll make it worth your while."

From the way she spoke Slocum wasn't sure how she meant that. The night they had spent together on the canyon rim overlooking Moab had been special, but he thought there was a deeper undercurrent in her offer. Money? Something more?

"I'm too close to getting the gold back," Slocum said. "And Sanders and his gang are responsible for three murders."

"If they sell Welkin's rifles to the Crow, they'll be responsible for more than that. Utah will explode in a new Indian war that'll make the fight against the Sioux pale in comparison."

"Seems there might be more than one way of stopping the uprising," Slocum said. "No gold means no rifles will be delivered."

"Welkin is a clever bastard. He'll find another buyer."

"But that'll take time, and I'll have returned the stolen gold to Wells Fargo."

"Do as you see fit," Helen said angrily. "I'm going to catch Welkin."

"You can't tangle with him all by yourself," Slocum said. The set to the woman's body told him he wasn't getting through her anger with this logical argument. "These are real desperadoes. They'd as soon kill you as look at you—or worse."

"Then come with me to catch Welkin."

"The gold," Slocum said. "It was taken from under my nose. If you catch Welkin and Sanders hears of it, then he'll move the gold and I'll never get it back. I have to go after what was taken from the stage."

"Watch your back better, then," Helen said angrily, pushing past him.

Slocum grabbed for her, but she agilely dodged and slipped from the narrow crevice back into the broader valley. In a flash Helen mounted and rode upriver after Hugh Welkin.

Slocum watched her dark silhouette vanish into the night. He cursed himself for being such a fool, but she had shown that she could take care of herself. Moreover, her chances of finding Welkin were slim. Helen might ride into the Crow raiding party, but it wouldn't much matter if Slocum were with her. Tangling with Blue Claw meant death to any white eyes.

He started riding back in the direction of the outlaws' camp, circumspect and alert for Sanders and his gang. Slocum paused to stare at the dead outlaw. Sanders hadn't even bothered to bury the man who had ridden with him as a partner.

Slocum hesitated, wondering if Helen was right about capturing Hugh Welkin first. Then he put it out of his mind. There wasn't any evidence against Welkin, other than what Slocum had overheard. If he captured Ray Sanders, the outlaw leader might spill his guts about the gun-running. An added bonus was Slocum recovering the gold, gold that would never go to supply rifles for the renegade Crow.

He rode faster, firm in his resolve. Slocum reached the outlaw camp and saw they had abandoned it permanently. It took a few minutes for him to pick up their trail by deciphering the faint clues he found in the dark. Sanders and his gang had started downriver, heard the shot that had killed the man guarding their backs, reversed their course and gone to check on the gunshot. As far as Slocum could tell, they hadn't bothered looking for either

him or Helen. They had simply left their confederate
where he had fallen and taken off. To get the gold?

Slocum hoped so.

He wondered if Sanders was the kind who would leave
behind a few men to snipe at any pursuers, then decided
the gunrunner would need a silver tongue and the cunning
of a fox to convince his remaining men he wasn't trying
to deal them out of their share of the gold. They'd insist
on riding with him to fetch the gold, especially Marley.
From the way he argued with Sanders, he had no fear of
his boss.

Picking up the pace, Slocum rode fast and almost
missed the spot where Sanders and the others had left the
river valley. False dawn turned the sky pink and gray,
then dimmed slightly before bringing real dawn to the
canyon. The outlaws' trail led down a side canyon with
its own tributary feeding the rush of the Colorado.

Once he got away from the river, Slocum might as well
have been following a drunk singing at the top of his
lungs and throwing away empty whiskey bottles to mark
the path. The trail was so obvious that he began worrying
that Sanders was setting a trap. Then Slocum decided the
outlaw leader had come to the same conclusion he had.
Speed counted for more than secrecy.

Slocum tried to keep the lay of the land in mind as he
rode, but the twisting canyons were too complicated for
him to maintain a good idea where he headed. It hardly
mattered. All he needed to do was follow Ray Sanders
and take the gold from him.

This suddenly became harder for Slocum when he
heard horses ahead—too many horses. He reined back and
looked for a spot to hide, thinking he had run afoul of the
Crow war party again.

"There! Fire!" came the echoing command.

The words had barely died when the reports from a
dozen rifles filled the canyon with their earsplitting roar.

Hot lead winged past Slocum, forcing him to retreat.

As he galloped away, more bullets sailed past him. Slocum bent forward, head near the straining horse's neck. He wanted to turn and wave his bandanna in surrender, but there wasn't any way the cavalry patrol was going to stop shooting. The soldiers were probably hunting for Blue Claw and were too spooked to pay much attention to their target, especially if their officer had ordered them to fire.

When his horse began to falter, Slocum cut off the trail he had followed all morning. He knew better than to run the horse into the ground. If he ended up on foot again, sore feet would be the least of his worries. Slowing, Slocum finally jumped to the ground and dragged on the reins to get the horse into a small stand of cottonwoods where he might hide.

Slocum chewed his lower lip as the patrol came galloping up. Their horses were in worse condition than his, lathered and broken down so much that they stumbled along the trail. The lieutenant leading the squad was sunburned and had a wild look about him. Slocum figured he was a shavetail on his first real patrol and was scared to death. The officer waved his pistol around above his head, issuing contradictory orders that his older, more experienced sergeant ignored.

"Sergeant Tompkins! Where'd that varmint go? He upped and vanished like smoke," the lieutenant cried out.

"You want the men to hunt for his trail?" asked the sergeant.

"That'll take too long. If they don't get on him right away, he'll get away."

"Sir, if we don't look for him he's sure to get away," said Sergeant Tompkins.

Slocum cursed the older noncom's good sense. If the young lieutenant had his way, he would send his men galloping all the way back to the Colorado River in a wild-goose chase.

"The captain'll skin me alive if I don't catch at least one of them gunrunners," the lieutenant said. "There's no telling what he'd do if he finds out I *lost* one of them."

Slocum caught his breath and held it until his chest threatened to explode. The Army knew Hugh Welkin was out here selling firearms. From what the lieutenant said, there might be a full company of troopers prowling around the canyons. Slocum had more than a plateful of people to avoid. A Crow war party, Ray Sanders and his gang, Marshal Yarrow, and now cavalry soldiers intent on bringing in gunrunners—any of them would cheerfully ventilate Slocum's hide.

He watched as Sergeant Tompkins dismounted his men to search for spoor. Slocum tugged gently on his horse's reins and began edging away. By the time the soldiers found his trail, he intended to be well past them, back on the trail, after Sanders and his gang.

Gold.

The glittering metal had become an obsession almost as great as revenge for putting him through such hell. Slocum had done his share of robbing and shooting, but he didn't cotton at all to taking the rap for crimes he had not committed. Ray Sanders and the road agents with him were going to pay.

Slocum climbed back into the saddle when he had gone several hundred yards on foot, leaving the troopers behind him to find his trail. No matter how good the men might be, their commander was too green to do things right. Slocum could find Sanders and the gold before the soldiers had doubled around and caught up with him again.

He rode steadily, chaffing at how the cavalry horses had chopped up the vegetation along the trail. Still, Slocum thought he picked up the faint signs of the Sanders gang entering a branching canyon.

He tried once more to get his bearings, and finally gave up. Wind and water had cut meandering canyons five hundred feet deep. He had to go on instinct.

Instinct did nothing to save him as he rode close to one canyon wall and a thundering roar filled his ears. Seconds later, the concussion knocked him from his horse. Slocum scrambled frantically when he saw the cliff face overhead erupt and bring down huge hunks of rock.

Someone had fired a mountain howitzer.

9

The ground shook and then the sky fell in huge, heavy chunks on Slocum's head. He doubled up and tried to get out of the rock shower, but was only partly successful. Rocks the size of his fists hammered at him before the real cascade began. Slocum was crushed flat under the weight of the debris but he fought hard, never giving up, finally getting on his hands and knees to scramble as fast as he could away from the plummeting rocks. An eternity crept by before he pressed hard against the canyon wall, avoiding the worst of the avalanche.

Choking on the dust, Slocum waited for the rock to stop falling. The worst of the boulders tumbled out and away from the wall where he cowered, leaving him cut and bruised from smaller shards but unscathed from the ones that could have killed him. Slowly, the rumbling from the breaking stone canyon wall died away and the sound of fallen rock echoed into the distance. Slocum swiped at his eyes and got enough grit away to see.

Riding up fast were a dozen blue-uniformed cavalry troopers. Slocum shook off the dust and pushed through the rubble to stand on shaky legs. He knew he ought to lie doggo but wasn't thinking straight.

"Get your hands up," shouted the officer decked out in gold braid. Captain's bars gleamed on his shoulders. "If he tries anything, shoot him where he stands," he snapped, half turning in the saddle to give the command to his sergeant.

"Right, sir," muttered the noncom, a stocky man who looked as if he had been through a war or two that day.

"Captain?" Slocum stumbled through the broken rock and fell repeatedly until he reached a level spot. He kept his hands away from his six-shooter. He might have been shaken up by having a howitzer shell blow away half the canyon wall above him, but there was no mistaking the squad of soldiers with rifles pointed at him.

He cursed his bad luck almost being caught by the shavetail lieutenant, only to blunder into the main body of troopers. Slocum knew his chances of talking his way to freedom would have been better with the greenhorn lieutenant.

"Who are you?"

"Somebody you shot a cannon at," Slocum said, getting back his wits. His ears still rang but he was recovering now, and torrential anger rose in him like water after a spring downpour. "I was riding along and all of a sudden I hear a roar and the side of the canyon falls on me."

"You're not supposed to be here," the captain said sternly.

"It's a free country. Why are you using this canyon for target practice?"

The captain motioned for his soldiers to relax their aim. Rifles lifted away from Slocum, but he didn't feel much better. The nicks and cuts from sharp-edged rock began to sting now, and Slocum knew he wasn't going anywhere unless the captain approved.

"We're scouting for a Crow war party. Have you seen any Indians?"

Slocum shook his head, covering his mouth with his

hand as he wiped away more grit. He spat and wanted to take a long pull from the canteen the captain had slung over his saddle, but he said nothing.

"Very well," the captain said slowly. "Tell me. How's Ray Sanders doing these days? You know him, don't you?"

Slocum shook his head again, remembering how the lieutenant had chased him, believing him to be one of the gunrunners. The cavalry must be splitting their duty between catching the men supplying the Crow with rifles and chasing off the Indians. He didn't envy them, but he didn't feel much sympathy for them at the moment, either.

"Ride with us, mister. Sergeant Bowdin, make sure he stays close. Understand?"

"Yes, sir!" barked the noncom. Bowdin unfastened the flap holding his six-shooter in its holster and rested his hand on it, not drawing but looking as if he wanted to shoot Slocum where he stood. Slocum considered it a piece of luck no one asked to take his ebony-handled six-gun. He made sure he kept his hands away from it, just so he wouldn't rile any of the soldiers.

"I don't mind riding with you, if you're going my way," Slocum lied. He wanted to get as far from the bluecoats as he could, but coming out and saying it would only raise more suspicion.

"Our way *is* your way," Sergeant Bowdin said. A private had chased down Slocum's horse and brought it back. The noncom pointed, and Slocum got into the saddle, aware of every ache and pain in his body.

Slocum found himself boxed in by four soldiers. The sergeant rode at his right side, watching him warily.

"What's all the artillery for? If you're scouting for Indians, dragging a heavy howitzer around must hold you back something fierce," Slocum said.

The sergeant shook his head and looked as if he had bitten into something sour.

"I don't ask no more. Captain Kernberg's never taken kindly to anyone questioning his orders. We done some strange things over the past couple months, and this ain't nowhere near the top."

They rode back in the direction Slocum had come. He hoped they wouldn't join forces with the young lieutenant. That officer had to find someone to turn over to his strict senior officer and was likely to point an accusing finger at Slocum. It would be even worse if the lieutenant's noncom had actually found the trail and followed it. Slocum would get himself branded a gunrunner for sure.

"There must be a company or more of you in the field if you've got a howitzer."

"Don't go askin' questions, mister," the sergeant said sharply. "You just ride and do what you're told."

"Are you taking me to your post?"

"I wish we was," the sergeant said, not telling Slocum to hush in spite of his order not to be too inquisitive. "We just got into the field and ain't likely to head home for another month."

Slocum looked around and saw that their horses were in poor condition but that their equipment was polished with the look of a long garrison stay. The rifles were new, and from the way the troopers' saddlebags bounced, they were loaded with ammo and food.

"We'll join up with the rest of our command and then figure what to do with you," the sergeant said.

Slocum wanted to ask more questions but saw that he wasn't likely to be answered. With the addition of four caissons and two mountain howitzers on their carriages an hour later, Slocum guessed that Kernberg had been ordered to establish a temporary camp somewhere in the winding Utah canyons, possibly to go after Ray Sanders and his gang, but more likely to stop Blue Claw.

By the time they reached the canyon where Slocum had eluded the lieutenant, he was getting antsy. His sharp eyes spotted the riders coming before anyone else in the company of bluecoats around him.

He hunched down, as if he had a stomach pain. The sergeant started to ask, then saw the lieutenant riding up at a dead gallop. The noncom passed the word along to the captain, who stopped the column to allow his junior officer to catch up.

Slocum was too far back to hear the lieutenant's report, but he caught the drift of it by the muttering from soldiers around him. The lieutenant had blundered across Sanders and his gang. Rather than tangle with the gunrunners himself, he had returned to fetch the rest of the command.

"Looks like we found the rest of your gang," the sergeant said. "Parsons, Dupree, Garza, watch this cayuse," he ordered, then formed the rest of the men into a double column and rode forward to get his orders from Captain Kernberg.

In less than fifteen minutes, Slocum found himself sitting on the ground and staring down the muzzle of a new Spencer rifle held by one of the privates ordered to guard him. The rest of the company had ridden off smartly, the lieutenant yammering and Kernberg trying not to look too irritated as they lit out after Sanders.

"This where you're putting your bivouac?" Slocum asked the young, frightened private holding the rifle on him.

"Naw, camp's ten miles up this canyon." He turned and looked longingly in that direction, telling Slocum not only where their main camp was but also that getting away wouldn't be too difficult. The greenhorn recruit was easily distracted.

"I wish we were there," Slocum said. "I need some food in my belly. Reckon you must be hungry, too."

"There's a mountain of supplies at the camp," the private said wistfully. "Food, even a crate of whiskey, though I don't think the captain knows 'bout that."

"That's a dangerous mixture to store together, rifles and whiskey," Slocum said, fishing for information. The private agreed, then realized he was fraternizing with the enemy and clamped his mouth shut.

"He's right about getting some victuals," said another of the privates. "You watch him, Parsons. Me and Garza'll go bag a rabbit or something. You ever et a roasted coyote?"

"I dunno," the young private said, not rising to the taunt about eating coyote. "Sarge said for us to watch him."

"The sergeant didn't tell us to starve ourselves to death," argued the one Slocum pegged as being Garza. Of the three, he was the oldest and had the look of knowing what he was about with his rifle. "I can bag a rabbit or two, we can get 'em cooked and eaten, and who's to know?"

"Me, that's who," spoke up Dupree. "Me and my belly! Let's go. Time's a-wastin'!"

Slocum tried not to look pleased at the notion of the two soldiers going hunting and leaving the young boy as his solitary guard.

"How long have you been in the Army?" Slocum asked. Slocum had been a captain in the CSA and had seen boys even younger go into battle to die.

"A month, sir," Private Parsons said. He blinked, realizing he didn't have to "sir" a prisoner but not sure how to back off from this formality now.

"Won't be long before you make corporal," Slocum said. In spite of trying to look stern, the boy was pleased at the compliment. Then Slocum said, "But I'm surprised you didn't notice that."

"What?"

"See the rear sight of your rifle? It's broken. You try to aim with a sight like that and you'll never hit a thing."

"The sarge has been ridin' me about how poorly I shoot." As Parsons lifted the muzzle to better examine the rear sight, Slocum moved. His fist shot out and caught the boy on the side of the head with a roundhouse punch that would have knocked down a bull. Parsons grunted and collapsed, unconscious before he hit the ground.

"Sorry, son," Slocum said, holding the rifle so it wouldn't fall over and discharge. He laid it beside the private, then fetched his own horse. The other two soldiers had gone hunting down canyon, in the direction taken by the captain and his company. Slocum had no choice but to go the other way, toward their camp.

Something told him that wasn't necessarily a bad idea. He vaulted into the saddle and rode off slowly, taking care to hide his tracks as he went. Neither Dupree nor Parsons was likely to be much good at tracking, but Garza had the keen-eyed look of a trailsman. Slocum rode in a figure eight pattern, then got his horse over onto a rocky stretch before letting it trot away from the three soldiers.

He hadn't heard any gunfire behind, signaling the hunters' bad luck finding game. The longer they took to bag dinner, the bigger the head start Slocum had.

As he rode, he settled his thoughts and tried to figure out what he ought to do first. Ray Sanders and his gang were long gone. His chance of picking up their trail was slim and growing fainter by the minute, yet the notion of simply letting them go scot-free rankled like a festering thorn in his hide. He had failed Wells Fargo, and three men had died as a result. If he had shot it out with the road agents, he wouldn't have felt as bad as he did right now. The gold was gone, but for Slocum that was secondary to bringing in Old Pete's and the two passengers' killers.

Riding around searching aimlessly wasn't going to capture Sanders. If anything, Slocum knew he was more likely to run afoul of Captain Kernberg and his cavalry troopers or Blue Claw and his warriors. And the good people of Moab had put far too much legal power in Marshal Yarrow's grip. The lawman might take it into his head to go after his first ever escapee.

Slocum glanced down at the hard ground and saw evidence of heavy traffic along this part of the canyon. So many horses had passed by recently that they had cut a double rut in the vegetation. Then he saw even deeper ruts, showing that supply wagons had also come this way. He slowed and looked around, trying to locate Kernberg's base camp. If the captain had two howitzers out in the field, he was likely to have even more firepower stored away in the camp.

Dismounting, Slocum walked forward warily. It didn't make a lot of sense that so much artillery would be sent into the field. A single howitzer had turned the tide of the Apache wars in Arizona. Why bother bringing more than a single cannon out here into the deep, winding canyons cut by the Colorado River?

Slocum was glad he proceeded cautiously. The camp was off to one side but what a camp! He had seen full-fledged forts with less equipment and supplies. Towering stacks of rifle crates set Slocum thinking in a different direction. Huge Welkin had said there wasn't any problem getting as many rifles as Sanders wanted, so long as the price was right.

These cases might be the rifles he somehow intended stealing from the Army. Two more mountain howitzers rested in their carriages, six caissons behind them. Guarding it all were fewer than a dozen soldiers, all with the inexperienced tenderfoot look of young Parsons about them.

Slocum crouched behind a huge mound of prickly pear cactus when he heard a horse whinnying. His hand flashed to his six-shooter, but he stopped short of drawing and let Hugh Welkin ride on. He hadn't expected to get back on the gunrunner's trail so quickly.

Slocum checked to be sure no one in the encampment

had noticed him, then slipped back to where he had left his horse. As he followed Welkin he got to thinking about how inept the soldiers were. It was as if Captain Kernberg rode into the field with a company made up entirely of greenhorns. Welkin had apparently come and gone from the camp without being seen, and Slocum had almost entered it without challenge.

Things were reaching the point where Slocum wanted to simplify them, with a bullet, if necessary.

Trailing Hugh Welkin proved easier than he had anticipated. The gunrunner hightailed it away from the cavalry encampment and rode straight for the side of the canyon. If Slocum hadn't been following closely, he might have missed the trail going into a deep fissure. He stopped at the mouth of the jagged crack in the side of the canyon and listened as Welkin rode through slowly. When the echoes of hooves died, Slocum entered and made his way along the tight enclosure. It spooked his horse a mite being in such close quarters, but Slocum kept moving until they came out into a broad meadow that looked to stretch forever.

The spectacular red rock walls, even when they had arches cut through them by wind and rain, had begun to wear on him. This was more like the scenery he hankered for. He could see the mountains all around, but it was a goodly five miles to the other side and everything in between was grass, trees and knee-high vegetation growing from the stream wandering along the floor.

He caught sight of Welkin galloping across the grassland and, before following, waited until the gunrunner angled toward a stand of junipers near the edge of the stream. Slocum checked his pistol, then took a deep breath. The time for action had come. He had been blown up and battered, held prisoner and delayed too long.

Even if Welkin wasn't meeting Sanders, Slocum was sure he could get the road agent's whereabouts out of him.

Slocum had seen enough men questioned by the Apache to know a thing or two about loosening tight lips.

He cut more sharply for the stand of trees, then weaved his way toward the stream and Welkin. Before long, the low-hanging branches forced him to dismount. Then, over the gurgle of the stream, Slocum heard voices. Loud, angry voices.

He tied his horse and approached on foot. With the stealth of an Indian he came within twenty feet of the gunrunners. From the number of men in the camp, it seemed Ray Sanders had assembled his entire gang to meet Welkin.

"You got the rifles and howitzers?" demanded Sanders.

"I surely do," Welkin said. "But remember, you got to furnish your own wagons."

"I want to see the rifles and the rest of the shipment first," Sanders said.

"Gold—we got to get that part settled 'fore you lay hands on them rifles," Welkin said. They began dickering in earnest, neither trusting the other but both wanting to deal.

Slocum watched. He was wondering how he was going to capture an entire gang of road agents and a master gunrunner, but something else also began nagging at him. He studied the hard-bitten men a few yards away from their boss and Hugh Welkin, then let his gaze drift into the wooded area beyond.

He caught his breath when he saw a white flash amid the rough-barked junipers. A face. It vanished as quickly as it had appeared, but Slocum recognized who else spied on Sanders.

Helen Murchison.

10

Slocum tried to warn Helen to keep under cover. He risked exposing himself to the gunrunners as he stepped from behind the tree, but they were already looking away from him—and directly toward the dark-haired woman. Slocum wasn't sure what she had done to betray herself. A small noise. A moment's carelessness moving about. Perhaps they spotted her at the same time he had, but it didn't matter. Slocum knew the fat was in the fire now.

Sanders and his men all slapped leather and dragged out their six-shooters. Slocum had a clean shot at their backs, but he had only six rounds in his Colt Navy and he couldn't bluff a dozen men.

"What's wrong?" asked Welkin, looking up. He was oblivious to whatever had betrayed Helen.

"You have anybody with you?" snapped Sanders. The leader of the gunrunners was on his feet, in a fighting stance with his six-gun pointed into the trees where Helen had vanished the instant she realized she had been spotted.

"No, I'm alone. That's the way I work. It's safer for me and I don't have to split with a—"

"Shut up," Sanders said in a nasty tone. He motioned for his men to fan out and come at Helen from the sides as he advanced directly into the stand of trees. The only way the spying woman could escape was to hightail it straight through the woods.

Slocum dropped back into deep shadows and waited to see what happened. If he tried to create a diversion so she could escape, he'd end up filled full of lead. All he could do was hope she got away—and if she didn't, he had to stay free to rescue her.

The thought never entered his mind that he could let her stay a prisoner. She had risked her pretty neck to save him from both the Moab jail and Sanders's sentry. It was his turn to rescue her.

"Close in. Fast. Go on, run, damn your eyes! What are you, all cowards?" bellowed Ray Sanders at his hesitant gang. As if responding to his own goading, he rushed straight into the woods after Helen. Slocum held his breath until Sanders came out a few minutes later, herding Helen ahead of him at gunpoint. She hadn't gotten far at all for Sanders to catch her so quickly.

"Who's that?" asked Welkin, confused. He put his hand on the pistol dangling at his hip, as if he were hesitant to use it. "You shouldn't bring your girlfriend out here."

"She's not my girl," Sanders said. "I'm not sure what she's doing here. Speak up, lady. Why are you spying on us?"

Slocum couldn't hear Helen begin her explanation, but the expression on Sanders's face told him that the road agent wasn't buying a word of it.

"Never mind the lies," Sanders said sharply. He stepped forward and slapped Helen hard across the face, sending her reeling. She fell to hands and knees and looked back at him, venom in her eyes. Slocum lifted his six-gun and aimed, ready to cut the outlaw down if he touched her again.

"You're an animal," Helen cried. She began sobbing, then curled up in a pile on the ground.

"You're not foolin' me, not for a second." Sanders swung around and stepped closer to Welkin. The two talked in whispers for almost a minute. Whatever Sanders proposed, Welkin didn't want any part of it, but he finally nodded. Sanders shouted to a trio of his men, who lit out like their tails were on fire. They quickly returned on horseback and waited for Welkin to mount.

"You know what you got to do," Sanders said to his men. He waved Welkin away with a quick motion of the hand still holding his six-shooter.

Slocum saw the four ride away and realized they were likely going to fetch the gold. Welkin would be paid with the gold stolen from Wells Fargo and the men would be shown the rifles.

There had to be more to it than that, if the rifles Welkin intended to sell were those still in crates at the Army bivouac. Those soldiers guarding the camp might be raw recruits but they were more than a match for only four men. Welkin had to get the gold but Sanders's men weren't getting the rifles yet. There had to be another step in the arms theft, but for the life of him Slocum couldn't figure out what it was.

He saw his chance at recovering the stolen gold evaporating, but he couldn't leave Helen Murchison in the gunrunners' camp for long. He knew what they would do to such a lovely woman. But he still faced nine men who had shown they weren't strangers to cold-blooded murder.

A dozen far-fetched plans raced through his mind. Getting help from Marshal Yarrow wasn't likely since the lawman refused to believe Slocum was innocent of murder and robbery. More than this, he had made a monkey out of Yarrow by escaping from his impregnable jailhouse. The only other place where Slocum might go for help against the gang rode in circles hunting for the gunrunners.

Slocum wasn't sure if Captain Kernberg would believe

him after he slugged the private and escaped.

With the marshal and the captain unlikely to do anything but throw him in jail and toss away the key, Slocum was left to deal with Sanders on his own. Besides, he dared not leave Helen in the hands of the gunrunners for however long it would take him to find the law and bring them back.

Helen's honor—her very life—depended on how well he planned and executed her escape. Now.

By the time the sun began dipping below the distant mountains, he still hadn't come up with any way to rescue the woman. Slocum shivered when he saw the bloodred cast to the landscape caused by the sun's long, slanting rays. If Welkin sold Sanders the rifles, the land would turn red with real blood.

The laughter from around the campfire lulled Slocum into a false sense of security where he hunkered down and watched. While the gunrunners joked around swapping tall tales, they weren't likely to do anything to Helen.

The sound of a twig breaking behind him caused him to snap to full alertness and swing his six-shooter around, ready to fire. The outlaw who had been posted as a sentry passed within a few feet without seeing him. Slocum was considering taking out the guard and reducing the odds a mite when he heard another road agent call, "Clay, you there?"

"Yeah, over here. What's up?"

"Just checkin', that's all," the other man said. "The boss isn't sure the woman was alone."

"Ain't seen no trace of anyone with her."

"Ray says he'd heard rumors of her and that Wells Fargo guard bein' in cahoots."

The sentry passed back by Slocum, but this time he stopped and sniffed the air like a hound dog.

"Come on. Let's get some victuals," the other road agent said. Clay sniffed a couple more times, then shrugged and moseyed off. Slocum sagged with relief, then cocked his head to one side when he heard the unmistakable sound of two horses' receding hoofbeats. Somebody had left the camp.

He swung around and flopped flat on his belly, trying to figure out what was going on. Counting the men around the fire proved too hard. They moved about constantly, getting up and going on patrol, while others came to eat.

A coldness settled into Slocum's belly when he realized that Ray Sanders was nowhere to be seen—and neither was Helen.

"When'll the boss be back?" one road agent asked. This cinched it. Their leader had taken Helen somewhere and Slocum had missed his chance to waylay him and save the woman.

"You know Ray. Once he gets a hair up his ass, there's no tellin'," answered the one named Marley.

"Damn stupid, if you ask me," the first outlaw said. "We coulda took real good care of her."

"He had to talk to them Injuns anyway. This is killin' two birds with one stone."

"You think they're lyin' to us about havin' a ton of gold to trade for the rifles? We'd be better off hangin' onto the gold we stole from the stagecoach."

"They ain't got a ton. The boss says we'll get three, four times as much from Blue Claw. That Injun's been robbin' and stealin' ever since he left the reservation. Gold don't mean nuthin' to the redskins, but rifles do."

"Reckon that means I ain't no Injun," piped up another. "I have a real hankerin' for a damn *mountain* of gold!"

Slocum let them begin daydreaming about the whores they'd buy and the whiskey they'd drink. He edged back silently to make his way through the dark trees to where he had tethered his horse. He rode out from under the trees and craned his neck back. A quick glance at the starry sky gave him his bearings. Guessing at the direction where he had heard the departing horses, he set off at a trot.

Sanders intended to give Helen to the Crow to help cement the deal of rifles for the gold the chief had stolen while on his rampage. It would be more merciful for the outlaw to kill the woman outright, because Blue Claw led a war party. They wouldn't keep a squaw as slave but would use her and then kill her brutally.

The stream running down the valley gave Slocum added help deciding where to ride since he reckoned the Crow camp would be near water, but he found himself cutting across the shallow creek several times because it meandered so. He wanted to keep his track as straight as possible to quickly catch up with Sanders.

Once Slocum got lucky and found fresh manure, showing he still tracked the outlaw and Helen, but by midnight he began to worry that he had lost them.

Then a slight wind whipped across the valley, bringing the unmistakable odor of tobacco on it. Like an arrow, Slocum fastened in on the scent. It had to come from the Crow smoking their damned pipes. He spotted guttering campfires within a few minutes and knew he had found Blue Claw.

Tired of sneaking around and spying without accomplishing anything, Slocum rode directly into the Crow camp. It was time to take the bull by the horns.

Four braves reached for their rifles but did not point them at him as he passed them. Slocum took this as a good sign. He drew rein and stared down at Blue Claw.

"I'm looking for Sanders," he said boldly. "Is he here?"

"You bring us rifles?" countered Blue Claw. The others in his war party circled Slocum, all clutching their weapons tightly. He wasn't going to escape alive—if he fought. So it was time for other tactics.

"Rifles and howitzers," Slocum said. "Where's Sanders? We'll bring you the guns after I talk to him."

"He go. He bring us a gift, then he go," Blue Claw said.

"The woman?"

Blue Claw nodded once, then leered. "She will last all night. We kill her in morning. Then we get many guns!"

Slocum considered a bluff and quickly discarded the idea. The idea that Sanders would deliver Helen as a present, then wouldn't give the Crow their rifles unless she was released, made no sense.

He had to use another approach.

"She is valuable. I wanted to dicker with Sanders for her, but she now belongs to you. I would buy her from you."

The Crow whispered among themselves. They had not expected this. If pressed, Slocum would have agreed with them. He had started talking and the words simply tumbled out on their own. Thinking through a plan hadn't paid off so he was running on pure instinct now. And it was working. So far.

"You give me many rifles for her?" asked Blue Claw.

"I'll give you real wealth. I'll trade her for horses."

"Many horses?"

"Many," Slocum agreed.

Blue Claw motioned for Slocum to dismount. Having no other choice, Slocum did as the war chief bade. They went to the low campfire and sat. It didn't take Blue Claw long before he pulled out a pipe, stuffed it with tobacco and began puffing. When he passed it to Slocum, this sealed the deal.

Slocum looked past the warrior as he puffed on the pipe and saw Helen tied to a tree, rawhide strips around her wrists running up to fasten around a limb. She sagged, almost unconscious, but she was still alive.

Slocum took a final puff on the pipe, then rose, saying, "I'll want her at sunrise. Alive and untouched."

Blue Claw sneered a little at anyone thinking the squaw was worth even one horse, then nodded.

Slocum was aware of the Crows' eyes on him as he mounted and rode from their camp. They thought he was one of Sanders's gang and as dumb as dirt wanting to buy what the gunrunner had freely given their chief.

All Slocum had to do was rustle up enough horses to suit the greedy chief.

11

An hour before sunup Slocum sat astride his tired horse, eyeing the way the outlaws had tethered their horses to a single rope strung between two trees. They should have been more careful but they had taken the lazy way out. And why not? Why bother constructing a corral in the middle of the Utah canyons?

It struck Slocum as comeuppance swapping the gun-runners' horses for Helen, but first he had to steal the animals. He drew his thick-bladed knife and slowly rode to the rope tied around a piñon tree. A quick slash severed the rope. He bent fast and snatched the end, giving it a couple quick turns around his saddle horn. Slocum rode to the other end of the rope, where the outlaws had secured their horses, and cut this free from the other cottonwood. He now had a string of horses, like he had gone fishing and caught them.

"Come on," he said, tugging on the rope to get the balky horses moving. They shied and more than one tried to rear and lash out with their front hooves. Slocum kept them under control but at a cost. He woke up the sentry who had been entrusted with guarding the camp.

"Who's that?" the sleepy outlaw called.

Slocum turned in the saddle, drew back and threw his heavy knife. The blade cartwheeled through the air and buried itself with a meaty *thunk!* in the road agent's chest. The outlaw looked down stupidly, dropped his rifle and tried to pull the knife free. Instead, he sank to his knees, then toppled over, dead as he hit the ground.

Slocum was reluctant to leave behind his trusty knife, but speed was more important now. He heard a few of the outlaws in the camp stirring. Of all the times at night, this was when they slept the soundest, but the combination of nervous horses and the challenge from the guard had alerted them.

Wheeling about, Slocum jerked on the rope holding the outlaws' horses together and started off at a brisk walk. The back of his neck itched, and he waited for a bullet to shatter his spine. Luck held for him. The few gunrunners who had stirred either didn't think anything was wrong or had fallen back to sleep, giving Slocum time to put a few more yards between himself and the camp.

By the time he forded the shallow stream the first time, he knew he was out of rifle range. The second crossing made his heart beat a little faster. The gunrunners could never catch him now, no matter how fleet of foot they were. And the final time he splashed through the stream made him think he could get away with this audacious scheme.

Common sense came rushing back when he saw two Crow sentries. Stealing the horses had been the easy part. Now he had to ride into the camp of a war leader as likely to slit his throat as to deal fairly. But Slocum had no choice if he wanted to rescue Helen Murchison.

"I bring trade horses for the mighty chief Blue Claw!" Slocum called to the guards. One slipped away as silently as a falling leaf. The other glared at him as he rode closer, the remuda trailing nervously. More than once Slocum had to tug on the rope to settle the horses. He worried the reins would come free and he would lose a horse or two, but he got into the Crow camp with all the horses he had stolen.

"You came back," Blue Claw said, studying him closely.

"I gave my word. A deal's a deal."

"Where are rifles?" the war chief asked.

"That deal's with Ray Sanders. This deal is between us. I have nine horses to trade for the squaw."

"She is strong," Blue Claw said. "Maybe nine horses not enough."

"Does Blue Claw go back on his word after we smoked a pipe?" Slocum knew the way to force the chief to honor the deal, but he ran the risk of angering Blue Claw, too. The Indians were as likely to shoot him down and steal the horses as they were to honor their bargain.

"Not enough," Blue Claw said.

Slocum knew it was time to play his hole card—his only trump.

"Sanders will give you more rifles, in addition to the horses."

"More rifles? How many more?" demanded the chief.

"One crate. Ten more rifles."

"No, not enough."

"With ammo. A hundred rounds for each new rifle."

"You speak for Sanders?"

"I do," Slocum said. He wanted to wipe the sweat from his forehead, but he forced himself to remain calm. Any hint that he was lying meant his scalp would be lifted immediately.

"You are a big man with Sanders?"

Slocum didn't bother to answer. Let Blue Claw come to his own conclusion.

"I want horses and *twenty* rifles."

"Fifteen," Slocum said, bartering out of necessity. It

wouldn't pay to give in too quickly. Blue Claw would know something was wrong then.

"We smoke a pipe," the chief finally said, after they had dickered for a spell longer.

Slocum grew uneasy as the sun rose over the eastern mountains and began casting shorter and shorter shadows. Time was running out, but he stayed calm.

"I must help Sanders fetch the rifles," Slocum said when it looked as if Blue Claw wanted to keep him sitting and smoking all day long. The Crow had a strange sense of time. They could become anxious and impatient in camp, but in battle they were patient hunters.

Blue Claw shouted something in Crow. A warrior rose and strutted off to the tree where Helen still hung. Slocum had cast a glance or two at her while he smoked, but she hadn't stirred. Blood caked her wrists where the rawhide had cruelly cut her flesh, but he saw no indication she was still alive.

The brave drew his knife across the rawhide and let Helen fall heavily to the ground. He turned and ran his thumb along the sharp edge, as if considering cutting Helen's throat as well as her bonds.

Blue Claw said something more and the brave shrugged. He cut off the rawhide strips and grabbed Helen by her long black hair. Slocum forced himself to watch dispassionately as the warrior dragged Helen over and then left her facedown in the dirt a few paces away.

Slocum stood and nodded brusquely to Blue Claw. He was aware that the Indians watched him like a hawk. If he made a misstep now, both he and Helen would die.

He grabbed her hair as the Crow brave had and lifted her face. Helen's lip had been split and one eye was blackened where she had been struck. But her eyelids fluttered and she tried to spit at him. When her blue eyes stared up at him, she jerked away in surprise.

"Come along," Slocum said, grabbing her wrists and

pulling her to her feet. "Don't talk, just walk."

"I—" Helen began.

Slocum jerked hard on her hair to silence her. This pleased the Crow and showed he knew how to treat a captive.

"No talk, if you want to get out of here alive."

He turned his back on her and walked to his horse. He heard Helen's painful shuffling steps behind him but did not turn to help her until she collapsed. Slocum caught her, then grunted as he hoisted her and dumped her over his horse's rump.

He mounted and turned to leave the Crow camp. Slocum caught his breath when he noticed Blue Claw examining the horses swapped for Helen. The war chief frowned as he patted the horse that had belonged to Ray Sanders. The chestnut mare had a distinctive white star on its forehead. Indians lived and died on horseback and could identify a horse better than they could another human being, or so it seemed to Slocum.

Knowing he dared not show any nervousness, he stopped beside the Crow chief.

"That's a fine horse, one worthy of a mighty chief like Blue Claw." The compliment distracted the Crow leader. Then Blue Claw grinned wolfishly and laughed. He knew whose horse this was, and it pleased him to think he had swapped for Sanders's property.

Slocum put his heels to his horse's flanks and trotted from camp. It wouldn't take Blue Claw long to remember there were fifteen rifles added to the exchange, and he wasn't likely to collect from a man whose horse had been stolen. Sanders would think the Crow had robbed him, and Blue Claw would demand the additional rifles.

It was to their mutual benefit that some deal be brokered, but if he couldn't stop it, then Slocum wanted it to take as long as possible. By the time a deal was struck, he wanted to be far away.

He turned toward the mountains along the western side of the valley and rode for several miles before reining in and dismounting.

"Let me help you," Slocum said, pulling Helen down from across the rump of his horse. She collapsed to the ground, looking liked warmed over death. Her pale face was pinched and her hands shook uncontrollably.

"Th-that's about the closest I ever came to wanting to die, John," she said.

"We're not out of danger yet," he told her. He splashed some water from his canteen over her lips, then gently touched her bruises. She winced but said nothing. He admired her courage. He admired it even more when she bent over and kissed him.

"Oh, that hurts," Helen said, smiling. She touched the cut on her lip. "But it was worth it."

"Blue Claw might take it into his head to come after us." Slocum quickly explained where he had gotten the horses he traded for her.

Helen laughed until tears ran down her cheeks. Slocum knew her reaction was as much relief at escaping as it was hilarity at the notion he had stolen Sanders's horses.

"That's rich. Sanders robs everyone and creates havoc, and you steal *his* horses. What's he going to do? Ask Blue Claw to give them back?"

"He'll trade for the horses," Slocum said, knowing what he would do in Sanders's position. "He still has rifles that the Crow want."

This sobered Helen. Every time he mentioned rifles and gunrunners it was as if he summoned up the spirit of a completely different woman.

"We have to catch Welkin and stop the deal," she said.

"Right now, we have to be sure we don't lose our scalps." Slocum studied the broad, grassy meadow they had crossed. So far, Blue Claw had not seen fit to come after them. When he figured out Slocum wasn't one of

Sanders's gang, his entire war party would be on their trail. All the gunrunner had to do was threaten the deal by saying Slocum was going to bring the cavalry down on Blue Claw's head.

"I'm glad I picked a good horse for you," Helen said, patting the horse's neck as she walked around it. "I wish I still had mine."

"We make do with what we have," Slocum said, but he agreed. If he'd had a little more time he might have been able to steal a couple spare horses. He mounted, then helped Helen up behind him. They rode slowly, her arms around his waist and her cheek resting against his shoulder. The situation was still dire, but Slocum found himself liking the ride.

"Why are you going in circles?" Helen asked some time later in the day. "We've passed that rock formation twice."

"I want to hide our trail."

"I haven't seen any pursuit."

"A bit of caution on our part keeps it that way," he said. Still, he was dog tired and his horse was beginning to falter under the double weight. It was early afternoon, but he had to stop for a little siesta.

He found a secluded area under a stand of cottonwoods where they were close to a stream but out of sight of any rider passing more than fifty yards away. Even then, Slocum spent almost a half hour carefully erasing their tracks with a bush he had uprooted.

"Are you finished sweeping up?" Helen joked. She looked stronger now, but her face still showed the ravages of all that had been done to her.

"Always was neat," Slocum said. He tossed the leafy bush aside. It had served its purpose removing all trace of the hoofprints in the softer dirt leading up to this oasis.

"Meticulous," she said, staring at him strangely. Her bright blue eyes danced with thoughts she was not sharing. "I need to get cleaned up. Will you help?"

"There's the stream," Slocum said. "It's only waist deep here so there's not much chance of being swept away by the current."

"I'm a bit stiff. I'm sure I'll have trouble removing my clothes—unless you help." She fixed him with her steely gaze. Slocum felt he was being commanded rather than asked, but he wasn't going to argue with her.

"Reckon I can do with a bit of cleaning up, too. If you'll help."

"Gladly," Helen said.

They went to the stream and began disrobing. Slocum dumped his gun belt and boots aside right away, then got distracted as Helen slipped slowly from her blouse. The sight of the twin mountains of succulent white flesh emerging from behind the tattered cloth made him respond until he was downright uncomfortable.

"Let me help," he volunteered. She turned from him, hiding her nakedness, but she pressed back against him when he reached around her. Helen let out a low sob of desire when he cupped her breasts and stroked over their sleek slopes.

She pushed back even more firmly into him when his forefingers and thumbs caught the hard red nubbins of her nipples and began to squeeze. Helen purred like a contented kitten, then reached around behind and clumsily fumbled at the buttons holding his jeans.

"Don't worry about that yet," he said. Slocum buried his face in the hollow of her neck and began kissing. Helen melted in his arms. He held her firmly, continuing to fondle her breasts. In spite of the grime in her hair, Slocum found its scent intoxicating. Or was it the scent of an aroused, beautiful woman that thrilled him so? He didn't take the time to figure it out. He wanted her as badly as she wanted him.

His hands slipped down her chest, across her belly, and

then went lower. He found the buttons holding her skirts and quickly released them. The heavy cloth dropped into the stream, immediately wet and tangling up around her sleek, slender legs.

Slocum let her turn in the circle of his arms so her breasts crushed firmly against his chest. Helen tipped her head back slightly. He kissed her on the lips and tasted blood from the cut. He started to retreat, not wanting to hurt her further. Helen would have none of it. She reached up and grabbed his head, bringing his face down hard to hers for a passionate kiss that sent shivers throughout his body.

Helen released her grip on his head when it became obvious he wasn't going to back off. Her nimble fingers danced across his back and went lower until she found the buttons holding him prisoner in his jeans. Slocum kicked and struggled to get them off without falling over.

"My, what is this?" she said, looking down between them at his jerking, throbbing erection. Helen quickly snared it in one hand and began stroking up and down.

"My well doesn't need priming on that pump handle," he told her.

"But it's so much fun!" Helen dropped to her knees, letting the water burble around her as she worked her mouth downward to the end of his thick stalk.

Slocum went weak in the knees when her eager mouth encircled his manhood. He stepped up and crammed a bit more of himself forward to experience more of her tongue and lips. Then she began tugging on him, pulling him down. Slocum sank to his knees and kissed Helen again.

With the water rushing around his waist, he experienced an unsettling reaction to the cold water.

"I—"

"I know, John," she said hotly. Helen stood, kicked free of her skirts and pressed the damp, tangled mat between her legs toward his face. Slocum clutched at the smooth curves of her buttocks and pulled her in even closer so he could thrust out his tongue in the place where he wanted to sink his manhood.

Helen shook all over, as if an earthquake possessed her body. She lifted one leg up and draped it over his shoulder, further opening herself to him. Slocum took full advantage, letting his tongue race about touching all the most sensitive places.

The beautiful woman sank back down onto the stream bank, this time lying on her back and lifting her legs so she could put her heels on Slocum's shoulders.

"Now, John. Let me guide you." She reached out and found his hardness. With a few gentle tugs she got it positioned properly, then lay back, supporting herself on her elbows so her face was just out of the water.

Slocum looked at her. He had softened a mite because of the cold water. Now he felt liquid iron turning to a solid bar of flesh at the sight before him. Her breasts barely escaped the stream. Twin red buttons bobbed atop her tasty snow-white breasts. Her belly heaved with anticipation, and the dark fleeced tangle between her legs was widely exposed. Slocum moved forward, found his target and wasted no time sliding forward all the way.

They both gasped in delight as he filled her.

Slocum stroked along the woman's legs, then bent her double as he leaned forward. This caused him to vanish an extra inch into her seething hot interior.

He slid back a few inches, only to find the surging water around his hips trying to rob him of his delight again. Slocum wasted no time sliding back into her well-lubricated core. He began short, quick strokes that caused a wildfire to burn in his loins. Helen began thrashing about in the water, gasping and sputtering and begging for more.

"Harder, John, more, give me more. Oh, yes, that's what I need!"

His hips surged like a machine that drove the fleshy piston with deliberate power and speed. He felt friction mounting, and the explosion that started deep in his loins erupted outward. Helen gasped and cried out in release as he sank full-depth into her. Her ankles slid off his shoulders, and she lay splayed out half in the stream, the water rushing over their privates.

Slocum bent forward and kissed the lust-taut cherry cresting each of her breasts, then worked up to her ruby lips. Then they rolled over and over in the stream, splashing about like two fish.

In the process of their passionate struggles, they managed to get some of the grime from trail and captivity off. Then both Helen and Slocum flopped onto a grassy stretch beside the stream.

"This is idyllic," she said, lying back and letting the afternoon sun filtering through the cottonwoods warm her naked flesh. "It's almost worth being held prisoner by the Crow."

"Nothing's worth that." Slocum lay on his side, watching the light and shadow play across Helen's fabulous form.

"You're right. But don't give up trying to make it better," she said, opening her eyes a little.

"Exactly what I had in mind." Slocum rolled atop her and began a slow, deliberate lovemaking that lasted until after the sun set.

12

"We've got to move on," Slocum said, stirring around midnight. He rolled onto his back and stared through the leafy shroud of the cottonwood to the stars beyond. The night was still and cool. Sound carried for a long ways across the valley, and all he could hear was natural sounds. That made him a trifle uneasy. The Crow were renowned for their ability to sneak up on their enemy without disturbing any of the wildlife.

He snorted in disgust at his own suspicions. The proof wasn't there that Blue Claw and his warriors had followed them. The Indians would have overtaken Slocum and Helen by now if they were coming. He suspected they still huddled around their campfires waiting for Sanders to deliver their illicit rifles.

"Why bother?" Helen asked dreamily. "It's so nice lying here beside you." She snuggled closer, pulling up the edge of the blanket to cover herself. The comely dark-haired woman failed just enough to spur Slocum to movement.

"You're going to lose that lovely tail of yours if we don't get moving," he said, swatting her naked rump.

"You're right, John. We have to find Welkin and—"

"Wait a minute," he said, sitting upright. "That's not what I meant. I'll get you back to Moab and—"

It was Helen's turn to interrupt him. "And nothing, John. Don't be ridiculous. I haven't gone through hell so I can go back to Moab. What can I do there?"

"I'm not sure what you're doing out here," Slocum said. "I'm after Sanders because he and his gang murdered three men, stole a gold shipment and I got blamed."

"There's no way you can continue after the Sanders gang," Helen said. She sat up next to him, holding the blanket to partly cover her breasts. Slocum found himself distracted but not enough to forget she hadn't answered his question.

"What are you doing out here?"

"Why, John, I thought that was apparent. I'm after Hugh Welkin."

"Something personal?"

"You might say that," Helen replied in a low voice. He noticed the set to her jaw and the way she clutched a little harder at the blanket. Slocum wondered if her grip would be any less if she had her fingers wrapped around Welkin's throat. He doubted it.

Slocum's mind raced. Helen was right about tackling Sanders and the road agents in his gang. Too many to fight. And if the outlaws joined Blue Claw's war party, even one of Captain Kernberg's howitzers wouldn't do him any good. They outnumbered him something fierce.

If he and Helen went after Welkin, there was a ghost of a chance they could prevent the middleman from turning the rifles over to Sanders—and Sanders would still have the stolen gold. That afforded Slocum another opportunity to wrest the gold from the outlaw. Even better, it kept the entire territory from going up in flames fanned by Blue Claw's war party.

"What do you know about Welkin and how he figures to steal the rifles? He intends to get them from the Army, but I don't know how." Slocum remembered the mountain of crates holding new rifles at Kernberg's bivouac. There weren't any wagons in the camp to load the rifles—and Welkin had told Sanders that he had to transport the arms in his own wagon. That was the reason Sanders had stolen the Wells Fargo stagecoach.

With a little cramming, Slocum thought twenty cases of rifles could be loaded into a Concord stage.

"You know something, John. I can see it in your face."

"Remind me not to play poker with you," he said.

"That's all right, as long as we can play other games." Helen's hand crept up Slocum's bare thigh. He slapped her hand. This wasn't the time for such distractions.

"I saw at least twenty crates of rifles in Captain Kernberg's camp," he told her. "And a couple howitzers. Kernberg had at least one with him in the field and another pair sat near the rifles, just waiting to be stolen."

"How convenient," Helen said as she dressed. "Imagine the Army bringing the very merchandise Welkin has promised more than halfway to the gunrunners from the armory at Salt Lake."

"It gives one pause," Slocum said, wondering who else was in on the theft. "I wonder if Captain Kernberg has been sent to build a new fort and needs the armament to support another couple companies of men."

Slocum hastily pulled on his clothes. After they had made love in the stream, they laid out their damp clothing to dry. This was the cleanest he had felt in weeks of dusty travel.

"There's no new post being considered," Helen said with great assurance. "Kernberg was sent to keep down the Crow and to stop the outlaws. He's not up to either task."

"What do you know about him, other than that all his men are raw recruits?"

"He's been court-martialed twice," Helen said. "Both

times he won acquittal, but he has few friends in Washington or in the Western Division left after the second trial."

"What were the charges against him?"

"Dereliction of duty," Helen answered. "He has a bad habit of ignoring his command in favor of firewater and soiled doves."

"The sergeants I saw with his command were veterans," Slocum said. "Either of them could be dealing with Welkin, and Kernberg would never know because he wasn't paying attention."

"Let's track down Welkin and ask him. Politely of course," Helen said, grinning more like Blue Claw than a genteel lady.

"How do we—"

"We find Welkin in his camp," Helen cut in. "I found it right after our paths crossed before. Welkin is not much of a frontiersman."

"You are?" Slocum studied the woman again, seeing more in her than ever before. He wondered what skills other than being an expert marksman she possessed. Besides the obvious ones, that is.

"I can outride, outshoot and out—"

"I get the idea," Slocum said, taking his turn at interrupting her. He grinned. "I especially like that last one."

Helen laughed as she gathered their gear and expertly stowed it while Slocum fetched the horse. He saw that the animal was rested, but having to carry twice the weight would tire it quickly. Unless he left Helen behind, he saw no way around turning this fine horse into a sway-backed mare.

"That way," Helen said with assurance, pointing west after she checked the position of the stars. Slocum had the feeling she wasn't posturing; she knew how to guide herself by the brilliant diamond-hard points in the sky and obviously had done it before.

They rode slowly until just before dawn, Helen ordering a few minor changes in the direction of their travel. But it was Slocum who caught the hint of burning piñon on the air and reined back.

"What is it?" Seeing Slocum's silent reaction, Helen sniffed hard, then smiled. "We found that son of a bitch!"

"We've found somebody," Slocum said. "These canyons have more people rattling around in them than most other Utah towns." From the faint scent, though, Slocum doubted they had stumbled across the cavalry. Even a small patrol would produce more smoke than this. The Crows were behind and Sanders's gang was miles south along the valley.

"It's Welkin," Helen said with certainty. "Remember? I found him before. He isn't far from a hidden trail leading through to the main canyon where the Colorado runs."

"Not that far from the Army bivouac," Slocum mused. "Could Welkin move twenty crates of rifles along the trail you mentioned?"

"No," she said. "It's too narrow for a wagon to travel. It's hardly wider than your shoulders." Helen smiled. "Of course you do have broad shoulders."

"He's on the move," Slocum said. He heard the *clop-clop-clop* of a horse walking away from them—heading toward the side of the valley where Helen said Welkin could quickly reach the Army encampment.

With silent agreement, they set out after Welkin, going through his camp and seeing that it had been abandoned for at least twenty minutes. Welkin wasn't far ahead, and he was going toward the rifles.

Slocum considered capturing Welkin and torturing the information they needed from him, but when Helen said nothing about overtaking him and sticking a six-shooter into the gunrunner's ribs, he decided to track rather than capture. Even with Helen's guidance, Slocum found it hard to find the crevice Welkin had taken. The vegetation grew down and naturally camouflaged the passage. He held back, trying to decide if he should plunge into the narrow fracture in the side of the canyon. Welkin could shoot them down like blackbirds on a fence if he heard them pursuing him. Slocum and Helen couldn't dodge or even take cover—they would be trapped like cattle in a chute leading to the slaughterhouse.

"Go on. He won't notice," Helen said. "He's too intent on the gold, the greedy bastard."

Helen knew more about their quarry than he did, so Slocum pushed on. The heat in the narrow confines was stifling and soon his shirt stuck to his body from the profuse sweat. The only consolation was the way Helen's blouse also clung tenaciously to her trim body, though Slocum could mostly only imagine it since she still rode behind him. Before he knew it, they popped out into the canyon, where a small breeze blew off the distant Colorado River and cooled them.

"Where'd he go?" Slocum stood in the stirrups and looked around. Hugh Welkin had vanished like mist in the hot summer sun.

"The camp," Helen said. "He needs the rifles and that's where they are."

Slocum settled down and thought hard.

"Rifles," he said slowly. "Welkin needs the rifles." He leaned over and studied the rocky path leading to the other side of the canyon wall. He saw some evidence of heavy travel, but it was hard to tell on such hard ground.

"What are you trying to say, John?" Helen sounded snappish now.

"I need to answer a question or two," he said. Slocum ignored her protests when he headed directly for the Army bivouac. Careful travel using the vegetation as a shield brought them within twenty yards of the camp without being seen by the inept sentries.

"Why are we taking a risk like this?" Helen asked angrily. She stared at the mountain of crates, all marked as containing Spencers. Just beyond, under a tarp, were boxes of ammunition. The two howitzers with their caissons had been removed.

"Do you think Kernberg has three cannon with him?" Slocum asked.

"I . . . I don't know. What are you getting at, John?"

"Don't make a sound. Just follow and keep a sharp eye out for the guards." He dismounted and secured the horse to a limb of a greasewood bush. Slocum took the leather thong off the hammer of his Colt Navy but knew he wouldn't use it unless he was faced with certain capture. The sentries were too green to waste ammo on.

Slocum motioned for Helen to hang back as one guard wandered by, almost asleep on his feet although it was hardly noon. The guard stopped to yawn widely, then slung his rifle onto his left shoulder and rubbed his right where the strap had chewed at his tender flesh. Yawning again and rubbing his eyes, the guard moved on. The heat wore on everyone, but more on this young man than on either Slocum or Helen.

After the guard shuffled past, Slocum went to the rifle crates and put his hand against one. He shoved enough to assure himself of its weight.

"What *is* it, John? What do you think you're doing?"

"I wondered if the crates were empty. Or maybe—" He reached down and picked up a bayonet one of the soldiers had carelessly left nearby. Slocum shoved the point between crate lid and frame and levered upward. The sound of nails pulling free should have brought every soldier in camp running, but they were indulging in a siesta.

Slocum pushed back the lid and looked inside.

Helen's mouth opened, then clamped shut in astonishment. Slocum had finally found something that left her speechless. The crate was filled with dirt.

The rifles had already been stolen.

13

"Halt! Stop or I'll shoot!"

Slocum ducked down behind the mountain of crates filled with dirt, hand resting on his six-shooter. It took him a couple seconds to realize that he hadn't been seen. Helen had been careless and let herself be caught by the indolent sentry.

She glanced down and shook her head, signaling Slocum not to shoot. The dark-haired woman stepped away from the crates, hands held up.

"Please, don't shoot l'il ole me," she said. "I lost my way and don't know where I'm going."

"Who are you?" asked the sentry, moving forward with his rifle leveled. Slocum considered jumping the guard but knew how dangerous it would be for Helen if he did. One slip of a nervous finger would send a .50-caliber bullet through her torso. At such close range, it would almost certainly kill her.

"Why, I'm looking for that darling captain of yours. Captain Kernberg. Where has he gotten off to?"

She stepped farther away from the crates, forcing the guard to follow her and put his back to Slocum.

"He's on patrol down by the big river, ma'am, but you

117

ain't supposed to be here. You got to check in with the officer of the day. And what are you doin' nosin' around our guns?"

"Why, are *those* big old things guns?" She turned and pointed away, causing the man to shift his focus. As he looked in the direction Helen pointed, the muzzle of his rifle followed. Slocum acted like a striking snake.

He rose, drew, stepped forward and swung in a single swift motion. The barrel of his six-gun smashed into the side of the private's head with a loud crunch. The soldier jerked and then fell to the side, unconscious. Slocum grabbed with his free hand and kept the rifle from hitting the ground with its owner. He didn't want it discharging and bringing the entire camp down on their necks.

"Well done, John," Helen said. "He'll have a whale of a headache and a dash of guilt but nothing more."

Slocum stepped over the fallen soldier and surveyed the camp. The sentry hadn't alerted the officer of the watch or been noticed by any of the other guards. Slocum dropped to one knee, grabbed the young soldier's collar and dragged him out of sight behind the pile of crates.

"What do we do now?" Slocum asked. "We've lost Welkin."

"Have we?" mused Helen. "He came through that passage from the other side for a reason. If he didn't come into camp, he must be meeting someone."

"Who? Where? We—"

"We have to find him," Helen cut in. Slocum felt a flash of irritation at the way she finished his sentences. He wondered if she was finishing his thoughts as well. If so, she knew how much it bothered him to be second-guessed all the time.

Slocum stood stock-still as Helen pushed past him. A smile crossed his lips.

"What is it, John?"

"I know where we can find Welkin." For once the woman was speechless.

Slocum stepped over the unconscious soldier and led the way out of the bivouac. In ten minutes they were well away from the camp, and in twenty they were at the bank of the Colorado River.

"So are you going to tell me why we came here?" Helen finally asked. She had ridden in moody silence, mad at both Slocum and herself that she couldn't figure out what he had.

"The sentry said the captain was on patrol by the river," Slocum said. "Welkin's around here somewhere—with Captain Kernberg."

"How do you know?"

"The gold for guns deal is about done. Welkin is probably getting the go-ahead to make the deal with Sanders. Welkin's not smart enough to do this himself."

"Kernberg's a clever skunk," Helen said, "but why do you think he is the boss?"

"He's at the end of his career and has to know it. He beat two court-martials and ended up with a command at the bottom of a canyon. He's not going anywhere, either in his career or otherwise. What better way to pension himself off than to swap a mountain of guns for the loot from Sanders's robbery?"

"I haven't given him enough attention, I suppose," Helen said.

"What's that mean?"

"John! There! You were right! That's Welkin and he's talking to an officer."

Sunlight flashed off the gold braid on the officer's uniform and buttons, but his face was turned away. The roar of the river kept Slocum from overhearing the men's words. Then Welkin turned and the cavalry officer turned with him.

"You were right, John. That's Kernberg!"

"Don't sound so surprised." Slocum watched from downstream as the men talked. From the way they stood Welkin was obviously the inferior. Slocum almost expected the gunrunner to salute when he stepped back from Kernberg and went to his horse.

"Who do we follow?" asked Helen. "If Kernberg's the kingpin, I want him, too."

"He's going back to his cavalry troop," Slocum said. "He's got a company of men roaming the countryside hunting for Blue Claw. Chances are pretty good he's not looking too hard for Ray Sanders, though." Slocum remembered how the captain had boldly asked if Slocum knew Sanders when he had come across him after blowing up half the canyon's rock face. The officer had wanted to know what to do with him. If Slocum had admitted knowing Sanders, he would have been let go free. As it was, Captain Kernberg had ordered four guards to watch Slocum, probably until the cavalry officer figured out if Slocum presented any danger to him and his gunrunning scheme.

"Welkin? He's going to where he stashed the rifles!"

"Where else?" Slocum said, agreeing with the excited woman. She clung fiercely to him as they rode after Welkin. Helen wanted him to catch Welkin quickly, but Slocum hung back, giving the gunrunner his head. Slocum had worried that Welkin might look back to see if anyone was following, but whatever Kernberg had said to him had lit a fire under his butt. Hugh Welkin kept his horse at a brisk walk and even let it canter on level stretches to cover as much ground as quickly as possible.

Slocum found his own horse tiring faster because of the added weight. He wished he had stolen a horse for Helen from the cavalry bivouac, but they had to make do with what they had.

"Someone's meeting him," Helen whispered, pointing

past him. Slocum had already seen the bluecoat coming out of a deep arroyo to wait for Welkin.

"I can make out sergeant's stripes," Slocum said. "I can't quite recognize him but I think that's Kernberg's command sergeant. A noncom named Bowdin."

"Bowdin? Alexander Bowdin?" Helen sounded surprised, but she wasn't half as surprised as Slocum.

"How do you know these men so well?"

"Be damned sure that's Bowdin," Helen said, her voice with an edge.

Welkin and the sergeant were talking, but the noncom vanished into the arroyo, coming back astride a horse that Slocum recognized readily at this distance.

"That's the shavetail lieutenant's sergeant. A man named Tompkins."

Helen Murchison sagged in relief behind him. Slocum wanted to find out what was going on. He felt as if he had sat down at a poker game where he was the only stranger. Some of the best advice Slocum had ever been given was to look around a table and if he didn't recognize the sucker, then leave right away because that meant he was the mark.

Right now he had the sensation in his gut that he was the only one who didn't know what was going on.

"Are you prepared to shoot it out, if you have to?" Helen asked.

"If I have to," Slocum said, "but fighting off Sanders's entire gang will take more firepower than's swinging at my hip."

"Take out Welkin and Tompkins and you'll have it. I don't think there'd be any more than them involved right now."

"What about the captain?"

"Oh, Kernberg's in it up to his ears. The entire command was recruited by him, so he knows who'll follow and who won't," Helen said with conviction.

"What's your part in this? You didn't happen to be on that stage by accident."

"By accident? Why, John, heavens no. I thought *you* were in the gang."

"Is that why you wanted to go with me when I checked the back trail? You thought I was signaling the outlaws?"

"Something like that," Helen admitted. "But I quickly figured out you were what you seemed—an honest man working for Wells Fargo."

Slocum could have disputed the part about him being honest. The opportunity had arisen more than once for him to rob a stage or train, and he had taken it, sometimes quite willingly. But this time his honor had been tarnished and he had to recover the gold and bring the road agents to justice, even if Marshal Yarrow stood in his way.

Slocum snorted. More than the marshal blocked his way. The cavalry captain and at least one of his men were also in cahoots with Ray Sanders.

"You never answered me about what's your interest in all this."

"John, there. Hurry. After them. They're going back to the valley. That must be where they've hidden the stolen rifles."

"And two mountain howitzers and who knows what else," he said.

"The Crow have been raiding for months, robbing and killing. By now they must have quite a sizable stash of gold to pay off Sanders, when he gets the guns from Welkin."

"Why doesn't Kernberg deal directly with Blue Claw?"

"I'm not sure. Maybe the Crow won't have anything to do with a cavalry officer. If they see a middleman, it'd be Welkin and not Tompkins or Kernberg."

"Makes sense," Slocum allowed. The Crow were on the run from the Army troopers. Even a crook like Kernberg would have a powerful hard time convincing a war chief he wasn't going to shoot him but only wanted to swap guns for the plunder accumulated by hundreds of Indian raids.

They slipped into the narrow crevice. Ahead Slocum heard scrapping of metal against rock. He made out Welkin chewing out the sergeant.

"Don't damage the merchandise. Sanders won't pay squat for a rifle with a banged up barrel."

"That owlhoot won't check every piece," Tompkins said in a grating, gravelly voice. "But we're gonna check each and every gold coin he pays with. I don't trust him any farther than I can throw him."

"I know, I know. You don't want him double-crossing us."

"If the captain'd allow it, I'd shoot the son of a bitch down, collect the reward on Sanders's head *and* take the gold. We can deal with Blue Claw. All I need to do is get out of this uniform."

"I'll handle the chief," Welkin said. Then the echoing words vanished.

"They're through the crevice," Helen whispered. "Hurry, John. We don't want to lose them. We've got to find where they're hiding the weapons."

Slocum snapped the reins and got the mare moving a little faster. The rocky walls were so close he couldn't really use his spurs. The heat mounted in the tightness, then a sudden blast of cool air warned him they were at the end of the passage.

"There!" Helen pushed down hard on his shoulder as she tried to get as much elevation as possible to spot the gunrunners. "That way. I'll bet they hid the rifles in that patch of forest."

Slocum agreed. The stand of junipers and piñons was only a short distance from the mouth of the crevice. Neither Tompkins nor Welkin had the look of a man willing to do any extra work. They had brought the rifles through the passage a few at a time, then stacked them nearby. It was a secluded area but gave a clear view of the valley sloping down to the stream.

"Sanders can drive his stolen stage right up, load it and be off to sell the rifles to Blue Claw in less than an hour," Helen said.

"And he can bring the gold to Welkin and Tompkins the same way. On the stage."

Slocum's mind turned over various schemes. He doubted Welkin would be among the living very long after Sanders delivered the gold and got his weapons. Tompkins had the look of a man playing all sides against the others. He might be in with Sanders and shoot Welkin himself or might try crossing Kernberg. Whatever happened, Slocum couldn't see Welkin getting out of it with any of the gold—or alive.

Welkin was the only one who could testify against everyone involved in the gunrunning. Therefore, he had to die.

Besides, why split the gold more ways than necessary?

A loud clash of metal on metal warned Slocum they were near where the guns were hidden.

"Tompkins dumped the rifles he was carrying," Helen said. "We've got to get there, John, and stop them."

"Here's my rifle," he said, pulling it from the saddle sheath and handing it to her. He knew she was a crack shot; she had saved his hide before with a rifle.

"Will you be able to get the drop on them with only a six-shooter?"

"Why not?" he said. "I've got six shots, and there's only two of them."

Helen laughed, kicked out and slid from behind him. She hit the ground and pointed to a spot behind a fall of boulders where she could cover the trail leading into the gunrunners' camp. He sharply turned to approach them from the side.

Any hope of sneaking up on Welkin and Tompkins evaporated when Hugh Welkin spotted him.

"It's him from the stage. It's Slocum!"

"Shoulda got rid of him earlier," the sergeant grumbled, reaching down for a Spencer. Distance worked against Slocum. He fired twice, both rounds missing. Then Tompkins fired the heavy rifle. Slocum felt a shudder pass through his mare and then it simply collapsed. He jumped free in time to keep the dead horse from pinning his leg to the ground, rolled and narrowly avoided Tompkins's second round.

"You see him, Welkin?" demanded the sergeant. "I thought I'd winged him, but I'm not so sure now. I know I shot his horse out from under him."

"I don't see him anywhere. You reckon there's more'n him out there?"

"Who else would be with him? Remember what Rafe said 'bout everyone in Moab gunnin' for him? Don't go gettin' lily-livered on me, Welkin. Pick up a rifle and get your butt over to those trees so we can catch him in a cross fire. There's only him, and I saw him before he could get the drop on us."

Slocum kept moving, staying low, trying to work close enough for his Colt Navy to be useful. The only heartening fact was that the two were alone in the camp. Helen hadn't mentioned the possibility but Slocum had worried more soldiers might be here to make certain Ray Sanders actually paid up for the rifles and didn't try anything funny.

The sharp crack of a Winchester told Slocum that Helen had opened fire. He cursed under his breath. She had been his ace in the hole. Now Tompkins knew he faced at least two armed attackers. Worse, he had forgotten to warn her there were only four rounds in the magazine.

Somehow, Slocum discounted Hugh Welkin entirely. That might be a mistake, but he didn't see the gunrunner as having the spine to stand up and fight in a shootout.

"You're surrounded, Sergeant!" Slocum shouted. "Surrender and we won't kill you."

"What? You'd take me back to stand in front of a firing squad? Or maybe the Army'd hang me." A fusillade forced Slocum low.

"What do you want, Slocum?" came Welkin's quaking voice. "We can cut you in. There's plenty to go around. Sanders is paying fifteen thousand dollars in gold for what we got."

"He stole sixteen," Slocum said. "He was rooking you."

This caused a moment of confusion. Sergeant Tompkins's attention was diverted toward the sputtering Welkin and Slocum moved fast.

He vaulted over a low rock and brought up his six-gun.

"Drop it!" he shouted at Tompkins, but the trooper wasn't going to give in that easily. As he turned to face Slocum, he pulled back the heavy hammer on the Spencer and tried to bring it onto target: Slocum's chest.

Three quick shots stopped Tompkins in his tracks. He grunted, lowered the heavy rifle and stared at the red blooms spreading on his blue wool uniform. An unintelligible spate of words bubbled out as choking blood filled his mouth, and then he died.

"I got him, Welkin. You want to die, too?"

Slocum saw Welkin walking out from behind a tree, hands reaching for the sky. Coming behind him, Helen had the Winchester leveled and ready to ventilate Welkin's worthless hide if he so much as hiccuped.

"Sit down and keep your hands on top of your head," Helen ordered.

"You don't have any right!" protested Welkin.

"You're under arrest for gunrunning, you miserable son of a bitch. The only way you're going to keep that scrawny neck of yours out of a noose is to confess everything."

"Arrest?" Slocum asked softly. Helen turned her bright eyes on him. She smiled just a little.

"I'm a special investigator for the Department of the Army. We got word that Kernberg might be selling rifles to the Indians and I came to investigate. Other than the captain, I didn't have any idea who was involved. But Mr. Welkin's going to tell me everything." She sighted down the rifle barrel at the sweating man.

"Tompkins, just him. Nobody else. Nobody but Kernberg, that is."

"Not Sergeant Bowdin?" asked Slocum. He saw Helen's reaction to the question.

"Him? Hell, no. Tompkins kept referring to him as a Goody Two-Shoes, always doing things by the book."

"You go along with that?" Slocum asked Helen.

"I'd better, since it was Bowdin who tipped us off."

"Wh-what are you going to do now?"

"You and I are going to ride to Salt Lake City, where you will sign a full confession. You might land in jail for a long time but at least that'll keep you from swinging."

"You promise I won't be executed?" Welkin almost blubbered now.

"Not if you give the federal attorney everything he asks for."

"I'll do it!"

"What about the guns?" Slocum asked.

Helen chewed on her lower lip, then said, "You can do me a big favor, John. Stay and guard them. Time is of the essence here."

Slocum knew it wouldn't do any good fetching the cavalry from the other side of the mountain. As long as Captain Kernberg was in command, their charges would be ignored—and they would be left dead in some dry arroyo.

"How long would it take for you to get to Salt Lake City and back with reinforcements?" he asked.

"Days, John. I need to drop Welkin off and then get a

detachment into the field, cavalry we can trust."

Slocum looked at the rifles piled up around him. Behind the waist-high stack of Spencers, away from the mountain of ammunition, he saw the two cannons. If this much firepower fell into Blue Claw's hands, the entire territory would become a cemetery.

"You'll be safe guarding the rifles, John."

"That's not what I'm worried about."

"I'll be fine," she said, giving him a quick kiss.

That wasn't what worried Slocum, either.

14

Slocum watched Helen Murchison ride off with a bound and gagged Welkin slung like a sack of potatoes over the saddle of his horse. Slocum felt at loose ends and not a little bit useless. The woman would clear his name once she reported to her superiors in Salt Lake City. All he had to do was nursemaid the stolen rifles until she came back in triumph and make sure they didn't fall into the wrong hands.

As he sat on a rock staring at the stolen arms and wishing he had fixings for a smoke, Slocum wondered how aggressive Blue Claw would be hunting for the guns. Of all the possibilities, this worried him the most. When Welkin didn't deliver the weapons to Sanders and Sanders failed to contact the Crow war chief, there would be hell to pay. The only winners would be Sanders and his gang, sitting pretty on the gold stolen from Wells Fargo. They might not make as much as they would selling the guns to Blue Claw, but they had ample gold stolen from the stage line.

Restless, Slocum stood and poked through the piles of rifles and then stopped dead, staring in amazement at his discovery. Kernberg had pulled strings all the way up the supply line to have been given a Gatling gun. Slocum had faced one on several occasions but had never fired one. He set up the tripod base and struggled to get the heavy multibarreled gun into place. It settled down with a metallic click. A dozen magazines had already been loaded. For the hell of it, Slocum shoved one into the breech, pulled back on the wood cocking handle and got a round into the chamber.

He put his hand on the firing crank but stopped short of actually unleashing the awesome power of the potent weapon. Now wasn't the time. The stolen rifles were hidden away from both Sanders and Blue Claw. Drawing attention to the cache would only cause Slocum trouble.

But the impulse was strong to fire a few rounds. Just to see what it was like.

He shook his head and turned his back on the Gatling gun. He had a job to do, no matter how dull it might be. Helen would return at the head of a column of bluecoats to take possession of the illicit arms, before the cavalry troopers swept through the valley to capture Sanders and Blue Claw and then place Captain Kernberg under arrest.

Slocum poked through the supplies Welkin had put aside and fixed himself a quick meal to ease his rumbling belly. A pot of coffee was quickly brewed, but as he sipped at the bitter cup, the hairs on the back of his neck stood up. Slocum turned and carefully looked down across the verdant valley.

Dropping his cup and going for his Colt in one quick motion won him a bullet through the hat. His floppy-brimmed hat went sailing as he dragged out his six-shooter and fired.

The bullet ricocheted off a rock but drove the sniper to cover. Slocum cursed his bad luck and set out after the man, clambering to the top of the rock for a second, killing shot.

He was too late.

The man rode hell-bent for leather away from the camp. Slocum sighted on him, then knew even one of the heavy Spencer rifles couldn't have taken the man out of the saddle at this range.

Cursing, Slocum slid back down the rock and looked around the camp. Then he set to work before Sanders and his gang showed up.

Slocum hoped an attack would never come, but he heard the clatter of heavy wagon wheels in less than fifteen minutes. He walked a dozen yards out of the hollow where the rifles were stashed and saw the battered Wells Fargo stage rattling toward him.

He had wanted to fire the Gatling. Now was the time to do it in earnest. Dragging the tripod with its heavy machine gun out, Slocum sighted down the barrel at the advancing stagecoach. He cranked off a few rounds to get the distance, elevated the muzzles and then ripped through an entire magazine as fast as he could crank.

The ear-shattering roar from the Gatling left him partially deafened, but he didn't care. He had put the fear of death into Ray Sanders and the owlhoots riding with him. For a few minutes.

He yanked out the empty magazine and stuffed a new one down into the breech, then cranked off a dozen more rounds. By now Sanders's gang had scattered, forcing Slocum to pan across the terrain, spewing bullets out wildly. This method of firing didn't even scare the horses; Slocum slammed in another magazine and concentrated the fire on the stage, sending splinters flying. He was rewarded by the frantic cries from the road agents.

"The stage! Ray, he's gonna shoot the stagecoach into splinters!"

Slocum didn't hear the outlaw leader's reply, but it didn't stop the advance of the bullet-riddled stage. Lifting the muzzles of the Gatling a little more, Slocum finished the magazine, raking the driver's box with a dozen rounds. The outlaw half-stood, dropped the reins and fell sideways off the stage.

"One down," Slocum said with some satisfaction, but he knew the battle had to go to the outlaws. They outnumbered him, even if he had superior firepower. Slocum loaded another magazine and learned the problems of a Gatling firsthand.

It jammed. He tugged on the cocking lever but could not clear the offending round. Firing as fast as he had had caused the barrels to heat and the brass of new rounds to no longer fit perfectly in the firing chamber. He jerked again on the cocking lever and then gave up, falling back to the camp.

Slocum was surrounded on three sides by boulders, but this worked against him now. He couldn't see Sanders and his men advancing until they poked their heads over the tops of the boulders. And to his dismay someone had gotten into the stagecoach and was driving it forward again. Without a horse, Slocum was trapped.

He went to one of the howitzers and began loading it. During the war he had taken over an artillery battery when its crew had been killed by federal fire. That had been a quick, dirty lesson in ballistics. Slocum turned the muzzle and aimed it through the gap in the rocks where the stagecoach had to appear, then stepped away, turned his back and yanked hard on the lanyard. The mountain howitzer jumped like a rabbit then belched white smoke and a length of chain Slocum had loaded in as shot.

The iron links rebounded from the rock like so many bullets, but only a few blasted onward toward the stagecoach.

"Get him, get him, men!" shrieked Ray Sanders. "Stop him before he can reload!"

Slocum whirled around, drew his six-gun and fired at the outlaw leader standing on top of the rocks to his right. The bullets went wide but drove Sanders back to cover.

The three gunrunners who had crested the boulder behind Slocum opened fire. He knew then that he couldn't stand and fight any longer.

There had been scant time to prepare, but Slocum had. A little. He scooped up a rifle and began firing until the magazine in its stock came up empty. He threw that rifle down, picked up another and slowly retreated through the camp to the second mountain howitzer. Slocum's mouth had turned dry when he realized how dangerous his plan was.

He fired until this rifle was empty, then shouted, "Come and get me, if you dare!"

Slocum clutched the cord attached to the howitzer and waited until he saw outlaws cautiously poking their heads up. Then he waited for another five count before pulling the lanyard. The cannon roared. For a heart-stopping second Slocum thought he had failed. Then came the second explosion, louder and more persistent. The shot from the howitzer had struck the stacks of ammunition piled to one side of the camp and detonated it.

Lead flying in all directions caused the confusion Slocum needed. He lit out like the demons of hell were on his heels. As he ran, he blundered into an outlaw. Slocum never hesitated. He lifted his Colt Navy and fired point-blank into the man's chest. The road agent gasped and tried to return fire, but it was too late for him. He was already dead.

Slocum vaulted the corpse and grabbed for the reins to the man's horse. The horse reared and tried to paw the air. With a leap, Slocum threw his arms around the horse's neck and held it down with his full weight. Kicking hard, he slithered around the horse's heaving body and finally found his seat. A quick yank on the reins and the horse was galloping away from the camp. Slocum made no effort to control the horse until they were almost a mile away and the horse's flanks began to heave and lather flecked its coat.

"Whoa, boy, whoa. Slow down. Don't kill yourself. I need you too much."

The horse allowed itself to be brought under control and soon was walking along as if nothing had happened.

The horse might have forgotten but Slocum hadn't. He wiped sweat from his forehead and looked over his shoulder, wondering if Sanders intended to come after him. Not seeing pursuit meant that the outlaw had taken all the beating he could stand. The Gatling gun had chopped up the stagecoach until it was hardly more than rolling splinters, and the last barrage from the cannon had destroyed most of the ammo. Slocum swallowed hard, then spit a mouthful of grit when he remembered what he had seen through the smoke and confusion back at Welkin's camp.

The ammunition might be destroyed but the rifles were mostly untouched. He hadn't had time to move them closer to the ammunition so they would be destroyed. Even a few kegs of gunpowder might have done the trick, but Slocum had been rushed. He had done all he could, and it wasn't likely to be enough. Ray Sanders had captured enough of the rifles to sell to Blue Claw and make his profit.

Unless . . .

A crazy idea came to Slocum, one that might get him killed, but he had to do something to prevent Sanders from completing the deal with Blue Claw.

He rode in a wide circle, coming up on the arms cache from the same direction as Sanders. He caught sight of the outlaws loading the rifles into the battered stagecoach. He cursed when he saw that they had already tied a howitzer to the rear of the coach. The Gatling gun was nowhere to be seen but might already be piled into what remained of the passenger compartment. It would be the prize offering to the Crow war chief.

Blue Claw might not get the rifles and ammo he had been promised, but he could get the most ferocious weapon the cavalry brought into the field. The only consolation Slocum took in knowing Blue Claw would have the Gatling gun was the lack of ammunition. Still, it would be a rallying totem for the Indians.

Slocum drew the rifle from its scabbard under his knee and checked it. From the rust on the exterior and the grinding sound made as he levered a round into its chamber, he knew he dared not trust the weapon too far. Having it blow up in his face would be worse than not using it at all.

Bending back, he made a quick inventory of the saddlebags and realized that this was a horse newly stolen from some unfortunate drifter. The odds and ends were all personal, not the kind of items an outlaw might carry. In spite of knowing the horse's owner was probably dead, Slocum had to smile. He had forced the gang to find new mounts by stealing them.

The rattle and clank of the stagecoach warned Slocum the gunrunners were leaving the camp. He got his horse into a trot and took cover in a low ravine. It wasn't much but he figured they weren't going to pay a lot of attention to anything along the way in their haste to get the rifles to Blue Claw.

Slocum's small sense of accomplishment vanished when he saw the stage roll past, the mountain howitzer and two caissons being dragged behind. On the top of the stage sat two outlaws with Spencers in their hands. Slocum simply stood still as the coach went past, and the two guards never saw him.

After waiting a decent amount of time, Slocum got his horse up the sandy bank of the ravine and determined the direction Sanders had gone. A feeling of determination came to him. He could still thwart them if he prevented the Indians from buying the guns.

It was all up to him. With that thought burning in his heart, Slocum set off to sabotage the deal.

15

One against an entire gang of road agents. One against a
Crow war party. One against Kernberg's entire company
of cavalry troopers. The odds were lousy but Slocum was
determined. He had no idea how long it would take Helen
Murchison to deliver her prisoner and return with enough
soldiers to make a difference. He had done what he could
up till now, but he felt a pang of regret for not doing
more. He could have been prepared for what happened at
Welkin's cache and moved all the firearms to the ammo
dump and blown everything up. There had been kegs of
powder for the cannons. He could have used them to better effect.

Slocum stopped berating himself. He hadn't expected
Sanders to find him as quickly as he had. While the easy
way was to ride like hell out of this valley, that wasn't
for John Slocum. He had never backed down from a fight
before and wasn't going to now.

He swung wide, trying to get around the gunrunners
and find the high ground. If they made the swap near
enough the canyon wall, he might bring down a small
avalanche on them. Slocum rubbed the back of his neck,
wryly remembering how Captain Kernberg had almost

buried him that way. But the corrupt cavalry officer had used a howitzer—like the one Slocum had let fall into Sanders's hands.

"He didn't have the gold with him," Slocum said aloud, coming to the realization that Sanders had intended to double-cross Welkin all along. That meant Sergeant Tompkins might have been in cahoots with the outlaw and tipped him off where the guns were stored.

As crazy as it sounded, Helen capturing Welkin might have saved his life. Given enough time, Tompkins would have put a bullet in the back of his partner's head.

"Damn," Slocum swore, seeing the stagecoach pulling into a small box canyon. There was no way in hell he could sneak around now, unless he made his way to the rim of the canyon. That might take a day or longer since he had to hunt for trail that might not even exist. The bright red- and yellow-streaked layers of the cliff faces were beginning to wear on him. The natural beauty, sculpted by wind and water, began to look like a poorly decorated tombstone to him.

Slocum saw quickly enough why Sanders had picked this spot to meet with Blue Claw. The howitzer was positioned on the hillside leading into the canyon, then carefully covered with brush while three men, acting as a gun crew, hunkered down to wait.

The men were unskilled artillerists and argued among themselves how to load and secure the cannon. This inattention to the trail let Slocum sneak past. He was in the canyon now, for better or worse. He found a spot to watch Sanders and the rest of his gang as they prepared for the exchange. Straining, Slocum could barely make out what the outlaws were saying.

"When's they gonna get here, Ray?" asked the one who had driven the stage away from the original robbery site. Marley was the only one Slocum recognized, other than Sanders. After he had winnowed the ranks of Sanders's gang, Marley was the only one who might recognize him.

"We need the time to be sure everything's ready for them redskins," Sanders said. He stepped out and looked around. Slocum froze when the outlaw leader's gaze fell squarely on him. For an instant Slocum thought he had been seen, but Sanders continued to make a full circle inspection of the area.

"Ain't none of 'em on the canyon rim. How could there be? Slim's just off to tell them where we are."

Slocum itched to look inside the stage compartment to see if the stolen gold was there. He doubted it, especially if he had been right about Tompkins crossing Hugh Welkin. All that remained of the upper part of the coach was splintered wood. The driver's box hung precariously and the top had been blown off by his Gatling gun fusillade.

The rifles were piled inside the passenger compartment, the barrels poking out the sides. Try as he might, Slocum couldn't see if the Gatling gun had survived the explosion and been added to the inventory going to Blue Claw.

"Just don't let anybody get an itchy trigger finger," Sanders said. "I don't expect the Crow to come with the gold."

"You reckon they'll try to cheat us?" asked Marley.

"Don't be a danged fool, Marley. Of course they'll try to cheat us. We sit on the guns till you and some of the boys go out to fetch their gold." Sanders turned and faced his henchman squarely. "You try to make off with the gold yourselves and I swear, there's nowhere you can run that's far enough to avoid me shooting you down."

"Aw, Ray, I wouldn't do nuthin' like that. None of us would. We're gettin' rich cuz of you."

"You can get a damn sight richer *and* live to spend the gold if you do as you're told," Sanders said grimly.

"Here they come, Boss!" shouted a lookout.

Slocum shrank back into the niche where he watched the outlaws. Blue Claw and a dozen warriors rode in, wearing haughty expressions and brandishing war lances. If anything went wrong, it would be in the next few minutes. Slocum drew his pistol and crouched down to watch.

"You have guns," Blue Claw said without preamble. Slocum knew this was incredibly rude on the Crow chief's part, and so did Ray Sanders.

"Good to see you again, too," Sanders said. He made a point of taking out fixings from his pocket and building a smoke. After licking the paper, he rolled it around in his fingers, then put it in his mouth but made no move to light the cigarette.

All the while Blue Claw watched impatiently.

"Where's the gold?" Sanders asked.

A ripple went through the Indians. They moved apart, arrayed so they could all attack at the same instant.

"Give us rifles," Blue Claw said in a sneering tone.

"I'll give you a whale of a lot more than that." Sanders took out a lucifer and struck it, holding it high.

Slocum almost tumbled from his hidey-hole when the mountain howitzer belched out. The echo momentarily deafened him, but it caused more than one of the Crow braves to be thrown from horseback. They scrambled to get back on their mounts, obviously embarrassed at being unseated so easily.

"Now, my boys up there with the cannon didn't bother loading in shot," Sanders said. "That was their first time. But now that they've got the hang of it, I bet the howitzer's got enough chain shot in it to cut you to bloody ribbons." Sanders put the match to the tip of his cigarette and began puffing, as if nothing had happened.

"You trick us!"

"Nope, not if you've got the gold to exchange for these guns."

Marley edged closer to Sanders and whispered something to his boss. Sanders angrily motioned him away.

"What does that one say?" demanded Blue Claw.

"He's says what I already noticed, Chief. That horse you're riding looks a lot like one I rode not too long ago. How'd you happen to come by such a fine piece of horseflesh?"

"I trade for it," Blue Claw said insolently.

"Who might you have gotten such a fine horse from? No, never mind. We all know what horse thieves Crow are."

Blue Claw stiffened. The knuckles of the hand gripping his war lance turned whiter, and he started to swing it around to impale Ray Sanders, but the outlaw leader waved it off indolently.

"Consider the horses part of the deal—if you've got the gold."

Slocum wanted to laugh. The horses he had traded for Helen had been recognized. He didn't doubt that Blue Claw rode Sanders's horse on purpose, to tweak him a little before trying to rob him of the rifles.

"We have the gold," Blue Claw said. The chief waved to one of his warriors, who swung about and trotted out. The brave glared at the cannon and its crew on his way out.

"Now, that's what I call a good thing, Blue Claw," Sanders said. "This way we both get what we want most. Hop on down. Check out the rifles. You can have the stagecoach but you have to supply your own team."

"That is not hard to do," Blue Claw said, sneering. "We have many horses."

The Crow chief and two of his braves went to the stage and began examining the rifles. After a few minutes, Blue Claw strode to stand squarely in front of Sanders.

"Where is ammunition? You promised it."

"There's been a little problem getting the ammo," Sanders lied blithely. "You take this shipment and we'll see about the ammo."

"We want it all now."

"Tell you what," Sanders said, seeing the brave Blue Claw had sent out returning with two others and three pack mules. "You hand over the gold, we give you all the rifles, and when we're gone, you can have the mountain howitzer up on the hillside, along with all the powder and wadding for it."

Blue Claw thought this over for a moment, then nodded once.

"Boss, this is 'bout the sweetest sight I ever laid my eyes on," Marley said, pawing through the sacks slung over the mules. "It's ever'thing the chief there promised."

"Congratulations, Chief Blue Claw. You are the proud owner of a hell of a lot of guns," said Sanders. He waved his arm and sent his snipers scurrying. He waved again to the artillery crew guarding the encampment, then said to Marley, "Get the pack train moving out of here."

"We keep mules," Blue Claw said.

"That's no trouble, Chief," Sanders said, obviously forcing down his anger. He saw that Marley and four others had slung the bulky sacks across the rumps of their horses before mounting. As he rode past Blue Claw, Sanders flicked his cigarette butt in the chief's direction. "See you in hell," he said.

Then Sanders let out a loud "yeehaw!" and galloped off, his men trailing.

Slocum saw the men at the cannon wait until their boss and the rest of the gang had left before slipping down the far side of the hill. Blue Claw barked out orders in Crow for the mules to be hitched to the stagecoach, then sent four of his men to the top of the hill to retrieve the howitzer.

Slocum found himself trapped in his small, rocky alcove longer than he wanted. The Indians weren't on the lookout for treachery now, but if he tried to leave they would spot him. Blue Claw would certainly recognize him as the man who had ransomed Helen and might want to extract a little vengeance for the disrespect Sanders had shown during the swap of gold for guns.

As the Indians left with their prize, Slocum worried what to do now. He had waited for a chance to stir the pot to boiling and get the outlaws killing the Indians, but it had never happened. Slocum had thought one side or the other would try a double-cross, but both Blue Claw and Sanders had been honest in their dealings. If trading stolen Army rifles and cannon for gold robbed from settlers could be considered honest.

Only a half hour passed before the Crow hitched up the mules and rattled off with their stolen stagecoach loaded with U.S. Army Spencers, but it stretched to an eternity for Slocum. Eventually, the last of the excitable Crow departed, boasting among themselves of their great triumph.

Slocum climbed down from his perch and found his horse where he had left it. Riding out of the box canyon, he saw the tracks and dust cloud left by the retreating stage, now pulling the howitzer behind it. Following Blue Claw would be easy, but what could he possibly do when he caught up with the Crow? The Indians were getting ready to go on the warpath and would be alert to anyone poking around.

Slocum wasn't looking to be the first white eyes they scalped as they began their war in earnest.

The only consolation he took was the lack of ammunition—blowing up the ammo dump had robbed Blue Claw of dozens of potential deaths.

Slocum found himself turning in the other direction, looking after Sanders and his gang. They had the gold not only from the Crow but also from the Wells Fargo robbery. He stood a better chance at recovering that than he did of stopping Blue Claw.

Besides, he didn't think Blue Claw would be hard to

find again. Just follow the stage tracks. Ray Sanders had shown real skill in vanishing like a puff of smoke on a windy day.

Slocum rode after the road agents, wondering how long it would be until Helen returned with the cavalry.

16

Twilight stalked the canyons by the time the outlaws returned to their camp. Slocum had ridden to one side of their trail, paralleling their course and trying to guess if they were going to make sudden changes in direction. Ray Sanders was particularly intent on getting to this camp and didn't allow any of his men to deviate from their trail by even a few feet. More than once Slocum heard the outlaw leader barking orders to his men not to straggle.

Sanders realized they were living on borrowed time now and had to clear out of the territory. Blue Claw would gleefully take their scalps—and get his gold back. And Captain Kernberg would be happy to gun them all down and eliminate a loose end—and get a mountain of gold all for himself. Ray Sanders had to know he had run out of allies in the winding Utah canyon lands.

Slocum sought to stop them, or at least slow them long enough for the cavalry to capture them. But how? He thought hard as he rode, and one crazy idea kept popping up.

If Sanders didn't have his gold, he wouldn't leave. Slocum didn't stand a celluloid collar in hell's chance of shooting it out with the gang. There were too many of them, in spite of the slow erosion in their numbers.

"The gold," Slocum muttered to himself. "How do I take it away from them?" As he rode, he turned grim, knowing only boldness would turn the trick. He tried to remember if he had been seen by any of the gang. The only one of them who might recognize him was Marley, the one who had driven the stagecoach away from the watering hole after Old Pete and the two passengers had been murdered.

But Marley hadn't gotten that good a look at his face. There had been too much going on, not the least of which being the way Slocum had hotfooted it around when the road agents inside the passenger compartment began firing through the roof. The sudden turn had thrown him off before Marley could get a really good look at him.

The glitter of gold could dazzle any eye, especially men as greedy as Sanders and Marley and their partners. That obsession might blur memory of a mere shotgun guard's face.

Slocum let Sanders get settled in his camp and start the evening meal, then rode as bold as brass.

All around him, hands flashed to six-shooters and rifles. The cocking noise from the weapons sent a chill up and down his spine, but he ignored it and rode directly to Ray Sanders.

"You the one they call Ray?" Slocum asked.

"Who's asking?" The leader of the gang stood with his hand on the butt of his holstered six-gun, ready to throw down on Slocum at the least sign something was wrong.

"Might say I'm a drifter just passing through these parts," Slocum said, his voice steady and his green eyes pinning Sanders to the spot, "but that'd be dumb. We both know that's not likely to be true."

"What is true? You got ten seconds before my boys here fill you full of lead."

Slocum spotted Marley out of the corner of his eye.

The man frowned but didn't recognize Slocum. If he had, he would have fired on him immediately. Slocum kept his body turned away to partly hide his identity, just in case.

"What's true? We're both in the same business, you and me. I traffic in guns. Heard you and a cavalry captain finished a deal so you could sell some rifles to the Crow. I can furnish better—and more."

"We're not gunrunners," said Sanders. "I don't know where you got that idea."

"A mountain of rifles and cheaper than the ones Kernberg's supplying," Slocum said. He saw Sanders stiffen.

"How much cheaper?"

"Ray, I don't like this," Marley said, sidling closer to his boss. "We got our money. Let's hightail it out of here, jist like you said."

"Pass up a big payday? That's not what I heard about you, Ray." Slocum saw that the notion of being considered a two-bit operator irked the outlaw.

"I don't give a good goddamn what you heard about me," Sanders said hotly. The outlaw cooled off a mite and asked, "What's the deal?"

"Mind if I get down to talk it over?" Slocum asked. He saw the way Marley's face screwed itself up into ragged furrows like some greenhorn farmer's newly plowed field. The man was struggling to remember Slocum.

"Yeah, come on over here and have a swig of whiskey."

"Ray, it's supposed to be *our* celebration," Marley protested. "We got the gold. We—"

"Shut up. We can hear what the man has to say."

Slocum dismounted and tossed the reins to another of the outlaws, as if he were nothing more than a stable boy. He hoped the outlaws didn't recognize the horse as one they had stolen. Slocum figured they went through horses fast, and after he had swapped their regular mounts to Blue Claw for Helen, the road agents had grabbed the first horses they found. Unlike the Crow, they wouldn't be able to identify one hunk of horseflesh from another.

"What's your deal?" Sanders asked as he sat on a log near the fire. A pot of coffee brewed, but the others ignored it in favor of a bottle of whiskey they passed around. Slocum was also ignored, which suited him fine. If they got liquored up, they wouldn't be thinking straight. He was playing for time—and their gold.

"Twenty thousand dollars," Slocum said, naming an amount that would soak up all they had stolen from the Wells Fargo robbery along with some they had gotten from Blue Claw. "I can get you a dozen field pieces, all the powder and shot you want. And five hundred rifles. Brand spanking new Winchesters. The ammo is a bit harder to come by for them."

"Where'd you get that many Winchesters?" asked Marley. "We haven't heard of a factory robbery. And they don't ship that many at a time."

"Been collecting them a bit at a time," Slocum lied. "Fact is, me and my partners have been stealing them by the boxcar load back in Chicago and shipping them out here where there's a big market."

"Not interested," Sanders said, shaking his head.

"I'd sell straight to the Indians, but I don't want to take that risk," Slocum said. "Better if you do it, you already having the connections and all."

"I can sell that many rifles for ten times what you're offering them to me for," Sanders said. "With that much difference, a man'd be a fool not to walk through broken glass barefoot to sell to the Indians. Why cut me in?"

"I have to move the rifles fast," Slocum said. "They were intended for a filibuster aimed at prying Utah loose from the U.S. Bunch of rebels who haven't forgotten the war, and Mormons, lots of Mormons, who don't like the way the government steps on their religion."

"Yeah, why should anybody in Washington care if a

man has fourteen wives?" joked an outlaw across from Slocum. "It sounds durn good, Ray. You think Blue Claw'd want more rifles?"

"He's got all he needs, but there are others who'd be interested. You remember Walks in Darkness? The Navajo war chief? We could sell five hundred rifles to him and his band alone."

Slocum sat back and let the outlaws argue over how much more money they could make. He tried not to stare at Marley, but the man kept his attention fully on Slocum. The brow wrinkled and began moving like caterpillars were mating under his forehead. Marley wasn't a quick thinker, but Slocum had the gut feeling he was a thorough one. Sooner or later he would remember Slocum's face.

"Can you deliver the rifles down south? Outside Canyon de Chelly in Navajoland?" asked Sanders.

Slocum stood and squared off, facing Marley. It wouldn't do letting the man remember on his own where he had seen Slocum.

"You. Your name's Marley, isn't it?"

This shocked the outlaw. He straightened as the thoughtful expression was replaced by one of stark surprise.

"How do you know me?"

"You shot my partner in the back, that's how."

"Where? I don't recollect any such—"

"On your feet," Slocum said in an icy voice. "Tell me why you shot Zamora without giving him a chance. Never mind," he said, cutting off his own tirade. "I know why you did. You're a lily-livered coward who could never face a man, that's why."

"You son of a—" Marley jumped to his feet and went for his six-shooter. Slocum was ready for him. Before Marley cleared leather, Slocum fired his first shot. It caught the outlaw in the shoulder and spun him around. Marley fell to hands and knees, winged but not dead.

As he turned, trying to raise his six-gun to get a shot at Slocum, Marley saw death in his adversary's face.

"Wait, no! Don't shoot!" Marley cried.

Slocum's finger was halfway back on the trigger. The smallest pressure would send a second round into the outlaw. If he fired after Marley had given up, the other gunrunners would avenge their slain friend. But if he let Marley live, the man would chew on that old memory long enough to get a little flavor from it, and Slocum would be dead within seconds of his accusation.

Slocum's dilemma was solved as Marley swung around and sat heavily. For an instant it looked as if he was giving up, then he hefted his six-shooter and fired.

Both shots, Slocum's and Marley's, sounded as one. There any similarity ended. Marley fell back on the ground, sightless eyes staring up into the gathering darkness. His slug had passed harmlessly by Slocum's head. Slocum fancied he could still feel the heat from the hot lead, but that might have been his imagination.

"Marley have any friends?" Slocum asked in a nasty tone. He looked around and didn't see anyone going for his gun.

"That settles his hash," Sanders said, staring at the dead outlaw. "Boys, everybody's richer by Marley's share."

This took the edge off and the outlaws began shaking hands and congratulating themselves for something they'd had no part in. When the bottle made a round again, Slocum was included. He took what appeared to be a deep drink but only wetted his lips before passing it on. The instant he lost his mental sharpness was the instant he died.

"How soon can you deliver the merchandise?" Sanders asked.

"Depends," Slocum told the outlaw. "When can I get the money?"

"You'd have to deliver down in New Mexico Territory.

The Navajo chief who'd be buying the rifles isn't likely to want to ship them on the railroad."

Slocum chuckled at that. "I've got a couple wagons I'll throw into the deal. They're not too reliable and might break down in the melée, but they'll hold together long enough."

"This is looking better and better," Sanders said, ignoring the flies buzzing around the dead body of his former partner. No one was in a particular hurry to drag Marley from the camp and bury him, and Slocum wasn't going to make the offer. Leave him for the coyotes. It was little enough considering all the outlaw had done to Old Pete and the two passengers.

"I want to move fast. Give me some of the gold right now to seal the deal and—"

"Gold? Who said anything about gold? I expect Walks in Darkness to pay for the rifles with Navajo blankets and silver. You know. Trade goods."

"Deal's off," Slocum said. "I need earnest money to pay a few debts. And it's gold or nothing. What would I do with a stack of old blankets, and there's no way I'm taking a wad of greenbacks issued by some Utah bank."

"So you expect me to pay you without seeing the rifles first?"

"You can see them, but it'll cost you." Slocum's mind raced. He knew Sanders had all the gold taken from Blue Claw in camp, but he wanted to tap into the Wells Fargo gold, too. Unless he got Sanders to retrieve that stash, he might never find it.

"All the guns?"

"I can show you all the cannons," Slocum said, "and one hundred of the rifles. It'll take a few days to port the rest down the river."

"Son of a bitch," Sanders said. "I never thought of that because the Colorado is so fast-running. But a barge could move it all, couldn't it? If you had an experienced river crew!"

Slocum didn't answer. He had no idea if it was possible and didn't care, as long as Sanders thought it could be done.

"All right. Tomorrow," Sanders said.

"Where?" demanded Slocum, pressing the outlaw.

"There's an oxbow in the river ten miles south of the cavalry encampment." Sanders blinked as if he had said something he didn't intend.

"Cavalry?" Slocum scowled. "I don't want anything to do with them. That's Kernberg's company you're talking about, isn't it? With us being competitors and all, he wouldn't take kindly to another man moving arms to the Indians."

Sanders laughed and made a waving motion with his right hand, as if shooing away flies.

"He won't interfere. Him and his green recruits are patrolling to the north, not along the river."

Slocum heard the lie in the outlaw's words. Sanders was playing a double-cross, but Slocum had to go along with it as if he was the stupidest man west of the Mississippi. Whether the gunrunner expected Kernberg to catch Slocum or had some other scheme in mind hardly mattered. Delay was the real game—delay Sanders and his gang from leaving with the gold until Helen arrived with trustworthy cavalry troopers.

"All right," Slocum said slowly, as if not sure. "You be there with the gold—I want it in coins or bullion." He saw this strike home. The loot Blue Claw had passed over was more likely in watches, rings and other trinkets stolen from settlers throughout Utah during the Indian rampage after they left their reservation.

But the stolen shipment had been in gold coin. Slocum remembered Wells Fargo Agent Riordan saying as much.

"It's a deal," Sanders said, thrusting out his grimy hand.

Slocum shook, wanting to count his fingers after to be sure the outlaw hadn't stolen any.

"I need to move some merchandise overnight," Slocum said. "See you at the oxbow around this time tomorrow?"

"Yeah, see you then." Sanders scowled again, took the whiskey bottle and finished the dregs, then tossed it over onto Marley's chest.

Slocum wished he could turn invisible and hear what Sanders said to his cohorts, but he had to ride out as if he intended to fulfill the promise he had made.

He rode for ten minutes into the darkness, cut off the trail and circled around to where he could watch the camp. He sat for another twenty, watching and waiting. If he had been Sanders, he would have set three or four men after him to find where the rifles were stashed. When the expected pursuers never appeared—and Sanders didn't ride from camp to get the gold coins from the robbery— Slocum knew everything that Sanders had said in the camp was a whopper.

Slocum smiled grimly. Neither had believed the other but both had played along.

Slocum knew what he wanted. Why hadn't Sanders gunned him down if he thought for an instant there was any double dealing? In fact, Sanders shouldn't have bothered listening to a single word of what Slocum told him. He was too cagey to play into another deal like that. All Slocum could think was that Sanders somehow profited from the charade, too.

17

By one in the morning Slocum knew Sanders wasn't going to fetch the stolen gold. He heaved himself into the saddle and tried to think up another way of getting back the gold while slowing the outlaws' departure for parts unknown. Sanders might have strung Slocum along hoping he would delay the inevitable flood of cavalry troopers to arrest him, but the gunrunner had shown no sign of getting out of Utah Territory if he feared his capture was imminent.

Slocum decided to head back to where Welkin had cached the rifles for Sanders, since that was the spot Helen would return to with reinforcements. For all she knew, the rifles and cannons were still intact and not in Crow hands. From there he could lead the cavalry to Sanders's camp and maybe catch all the road agents red-handed. As to the rifles Blue Claw had taken—that was a burden that would be on the entire territory for a long, long time.

Even as the thought that he might spin a new yarn to slow Sanders entered his mind, Slocum discarded it as ridiculous. Sanders and his gang had been mighty cagey so far. There wasn't any reason under the sun for them to stick around. He had waited for Sanders to go after the hidden treasure trove, but Slocum knew he might have guessed wrong about actually flushing the outlaw. Sanders might have all the gold in his camp where he could watch it. If true, that meant Sanders had no need to sneak away from the others in his gang to fetch the spoils of the Wells Fargo robbery.

The last thing in the world Slocum had expected was for Ray Sanders to be an honest crook and divvy up all the gold with his partners.

Slowly walking his horse through the night, Slocum found the faint trail and rode up the grassy valley with a wind blowing gently against his weathered face. Being under the stars, out in the open, let him clear his head, but he felt shackled by being outgunned so seriously and needing to pry loose the stolen gold from Sanders's grasping hand. Without both outlaw and gold he could never clear his name.

Slocum didn't give two hoots what Marshal Yarrow thought, but the Wells Fargo agent had hired him and he had sworn to protect the shipments and passengers. He owed it to Gus Riordan to bring in both the gold and old Pete's killer. Hell, Slocum owed it to Old Pete.

An hour after leaving his vantage point outside Sanders's camp, Slocum got an itchy feeling up and down his back. He drew rein and twisted about to study his back trail. Nothing stirred in the night except occasional clouds darting through the sky. The half moon was threatening to rise all the way above the distant mountains at any minute, but it cast only a pale, reflected light across the landscape. It was hardly enough to make out trees, much less any distinct shape—like a rider—that might be coming after him.

Slocum sat and watched patiently for more than fifteen minutes without seeing anything unusual, but the sensation of being spied on gnawed away at him. He cut off the trail and doubled back to see if he could flush anyone.

Nothing. He might as well have been alone in this grassy valley made for cattle grazing.

Slocum knew better than to dismiss his feelings as nerves. Over the years he had developed a reliable sixth sense that had saved him from some deadly situations. Dozens of barely recognized details probably came together in his brain to give him the uneasiness. He didn't know the process or what he might be hearing and seeing at the fringes of his mind, but he trusted his instincts.

He rode in a zigzag pattern for a couple more hours, but not a hint showed of anyone or anything behind him. Less than an hour before dawn he whipped his horse with the reins and galloped toward Welkin's camp. It was too soon for Helen to return, but he still halfway expected to find someone in the camp. All that remained was the gunpowder stench from so many rounds of ammo being ignited and the smell of wood and iron left after the explosion destroyed a few of the guns.

The feeling of being watched had not faded with the night. Slocum considered what to do and realized he would have to deal with Ray Sanders and his gang soon enough. If Sanders took the bait, he would be at the oxbow in the Colorado River early in the evening, but Slocum doubted the gunrunner would show up. Sanders had something else in mind for Slocum, so Slocum had to come up with another plan to trap the road agent.

Slocum hit the ground and began pawing through the remains of the rifles, pulling out mangled barrels. He spent the next half hour climbing into the nearby rocks, going into the woods and finding just the right places in notches on trees and finally sticking a few of the ruined barrels into tight crevices down lower around the burned-out camp. As the dawn broke, Slocum looked as if he were in the center of a firing squad. Rifles from all directions pointed down into the camp.

If only there were marksmen behind each barrel, Slocum would have felt a mite easier, but the sensation mounted that something was seriously wrong.

He turned and saw Sanders and three of his men astride their horses, watching. They hadn't ridden up the trail from the valley or Slocum would have seen them. Some other hiding spot nearby gave the only answer—and that meant Slocum's work placing the rifle barrels around was for naught.

"You mean to sell me these rifles?" Sanders asked. A sardonic smile danced on the outlaw's lips.

Slocum considered trying to run his bluff a little longer but knew it was probably futile.

"I mean to shove those barrels down your throat," Slocum said.

"No more playacting like you're the big-time gunrunner, eh?" Sanders inclined his head slightly and the three men with him went for their six-shooters.

He slapped leather and got his Colt Navy out and firing before any of the outlaws drew. Slocum's first shot took off one road agent's hat—and the top of his head along with it. Blood geysered backward in a fountain as the road agent lost part of his scalp to the .36-caliber bullet. Then the horses were rearing and bucking, making accurate shooting impossible.

Slocum hit the ground and rolled to come up behind a burned log. He rested his hand on the log and tried to get a good shot at Sanders, but the outlaw leader was struggling to keep his horse from running away with him. Another road agent fell heavily to the ground and fought to get to his feet. Slocum shot him in the gut.

Then the next four shots all missed their mark.

"I'm gettin' outta here, Ray," cried the one remaining outlaw with Sanders.

"Get your ass back here. He's alone. We can take him!"

"He done shot Grinnell and Jack. I seen how good he is when he cut down Marley back at our camp."

Slocum worked to reload. This gave the outlaw time to skedaddle. Sanders let his horse carry him out of range of a six-gun but didn't take off for the high country as his henchman had. By the time Slocum had his six-shooter ready for action again, Ray Sanders had a rifle out and was aiming it.

Although he was woefully out of range, Slocum fired. The slug ricocheted off a rock and whined past Sanders's horse, spooking it again and spoiling the outlaw's aim. The heavier rifle bullet passed harmlessly over Slocum's head.

"I don't know who you are, but you're a dead man," shouted Sanders. "You're no gunrunner, that's for certain, and nobody this side of hell's ever brought a barge loaded with guns down from higher on the Colorado."

Slocum kept low and ran to a tumble of rocks, hoping for better cover. He was closer to Sanders and had a better shot at him, but again Slocum felt a creeping uneasiness. Why didn't Sanders hightail it along with his remaining partner?

There was only one reason. Slocum whirled around, six-shooter coming up. He froze. He faced three rifles, all aimed at him. Sanders had decoyed him, kept his attention away from the rest of the gang as they crept up from behind.

"Kin I jist shoot the varmint, Ray?" asked the outlaw in the middle.

"No!" Sanders rode up, his rifle waving about. "I want to find out who the hell he is."

"Does it much matter? He got rid of Marley. Anybody who shot that son of a bitch done us all a favor. Least we kin do is return it by giving him a quick death." The man grinned and showed two missing front teeth. Seeing Slocum's eyes fix on the missing teeth, the outlaw smiled even more broadly. "Yep, Marley done that to me when we was drunk. Never forgot, never forgave. So I figger I owe you something."

"Don't shoot him," Sanders repeated. The gang leader dropped to the ground, came over and drove the butt of his rifle into Slocum's right wrist. The ebony-handled Colt went flying, and Slocum winced in pain. As he bent over slightly, Sanders reversed the direction of the rifle and caught Slocum under the chin with the steel barrel.

Slocum staggered back against a tree, his head spinning.

"Who are you? You work for the Army? The War Department? I heard tell General Sherman wants to crack down on the Indians. Anybody supplying rifles to them would be a prime target."

"Don't know Sherman," Slocum said, rubbing his wrist and then his jaw.

"You from Georgia? The way you talk says so. You were probably a Johnny Reb. No, you wouldn't much like Sherman, not the way he burned Atlanta and raped half of Georgia getting there." Sanders swung his rifle again. The butt struck Slocum in the belly. He was prepared for it, but the impact still caused him to double over in pain.

"What's the diff'rence who the varmint's workin' for, Ray? Jist kill him and let's get outta here."

"I'm curious," Sanders said. "He knows a powerful lot about us. I want to know how."

Sanders stepped up to Slocum and reared back to hit him in the face with the rifle butt. Slocum saw the outlaw's boots coming from his bent-over position. Sucking in his breath, he lowered his head even more and charged like a bull. His shoulder crashed into Sanders's midsection and knocked the man back. Slocum kept swarming and ended up on top of the outlaw.

He got in one good punch before the other three highwaymen grabbed him and pulled him off their boss.

"Kill him, Ray," repeated the outlaw.

"I'm mad now," Sanders said, swiping at his bloody, broken nose.

"I'm not letting him go to his maker without telling me everything he knows."

"That won't take more'n a minute, from the look of him," said another member of the gang.

Slocum hung in the grip of two outlaws, then sagged. As they tried to follow him down, he got his feet under him and shot upward like a rocket, yanking hard on his arms and freeing them. Slocum spun around, kicked out with his boot and caught the third outlaw in the crotch. The man shrieked in pain and dropped his rifle.

Diving, Slocum grabbed it, rolled and came up with the rifle covering the rest of the gang. He wasn't going to try capturing them. His finger came back on the trigger when he got Ray Sanders in his sights.

The hammer fell on a punk round.

He levered a new round in but had run out of time. The two he had thrown off began whaling the living daylights out of him. Slocum blocked one with the useless rifle, only to have the other pummel him from a different direction. As he tried to block the second man, he saw movement and heard the unmistakable sound of a cocking hammer.

"Get away from him," Sanders said. The outlaw stood with his six-shooter pointed straight at Slocum. His hand shook. Slocum ignored the bore of the gun and stared into the outlaw's eyes.

Sanders lowered the six-gun and said, "Tie him up. I need to know who he is and what he's up to."

"Boss—"

"Shut up," snapped Sanders. "We got to know if Kernberg has gone against us or if this yahoo works for somebody else. What's he know and who else knows it?"

"We can get out of the country, Ray. Ain't nobody in Mexico that won't take our gold. I kin do with a bottle of tequila and a friendly señorita on my arm."

"I have to know," Sanders said doggedly. He stared at Slocum, now bound hand and foot. "Tell me why you're nosing into our business."

Slocum said nothing. He knew what was going to happen, and if he said anything now it would only make the torture worse later. Sanders wouldn't believe a word of what he said, even if Slocum had felt the least bit inclined to cooperate.

"Good, don't answer. I might like this. You've cut down some of my best men."

" 'Cept for Marley," chimed in one of the outlaws. "I swear, if this galoot hadn't kilt Marley, I would have done it myself."

Sanders sat on a rock and studied Slocum like he might a poker hand.

"Let's see now. You knew this spot and rode right to it. We were watching you from the second you left our camp last night."

Slocum fumed at this. There weren't many men who were better at tracking unseen, but they existed. He'd had the bad luck to find one in Ray Sanders. If he had paid even more attention to his uneasiness out on the trail, he might still be free. Beating up on himself wouldn't get him free. He looked around, trying to calculate his odds of escaping. They didn't look too good.

Slocum smiled wryly, then laughed ruefully. He wouldn't have to beat up on himself. Sanders and his gang would do that for him.

"You're mighty good, if you followed me," Slocum said.

"I'm better than good. I'm the best," boasted Sanders. "You're not too bad, the way you rode back and forth trying to throw me off the trail, but I figured it out early on that you were headed here." Sanders motioned. "I never thought much on it, but you must be the bastard who blew up the ammo and ruined so many of our rifles. You came back here for a reason, though, and it wasn't to pick up a bunch of rifle barrels to try to sell me."

"You're doing the talking," Slocum said. He winced as both the men who had tied him up punched him in the gut. Slocum gasped out, "I'm waiting for an entire company of cavalry."

"Are you now?" asked Sanders, pursing his lips. "If I thought that, I'd kill you and hightail it like my boys want." He silenced his men with a look. "No way could I fight off an entire company, even Kernberg's recruits."

"What are you afraid of?" Slocum asked. He saw that he'd hit the target from the way Sanders's eyes widened.

"I'm not afraid of anything."

"Kernberg knows where the gold is, doesn't he? You're afraid he'll steal what you stole from the Wells Fargo robbery."

"Kernberg doesn't even know me by sight," Sanders said. "That's why I used Welkin as a go-between. I never trusted that bluecoated son of a bitch, especially since so many of his noncoms were willing to go against him."

"Boss, you think he might work for Wells Fargo?"

"He just might be an agent for the company," Sanders said thoughtfully. "That makes sense. He knows about the stage robbery. Might be he stumbled on the gunrunning and figured we used the stolen gold to pay off Welkin."

"Welkin never got the gold," Slocum said. His belly ached from the beating. "You kept it. You always meant to double-cross him, you and Tompkins. Just like you're going to double-cross the rest of your gang."

"Go on," Sanders said. "Beat on him some more."

As the outlaws punched and kicked Slocum, Sanders sat and watched. Anger showed on his face, telling Slocum he had hit mighty close to the truth. Sanders fingered his six-gun, but did he intend to shoot Slocum or the three men working him over?

"No purpose keeping you alive," Sanders said as the men continued to hammer away at Slocum.

Slocum heard him through a roar in his ears. He rolled to one side to protect his aching belly, only to take a boot in the ribs. Pain surged throughout his body now, making it hard to focus. Slocum jerked away as he rolled onto a sharp piece of metal, then rolled back so his hands were under him. He jerked and moaned and rolled from side to side, as much to avoid new blows as to drag the rope on his wrists against the shrapnel buried beneath him in the ground.

"Boss, somebody's coming. A lot of men, from the look."

Sanders straightened and shielded his eyes as he looked into the morning sun.

"Kill him," Sanders snapped. "Then split up and meet back at our camp."

The men who had been battering Slocum stepped away and reached for their rifles. As they did Slocum heaved hard and broke the strands of rope he had not successfully severed already on the shrapnel. His feet were still bound but he rolled onto his belly, pushed up and kicked like a mule, knocking one outlaw into his partner. Intent on staying alive, Slocum grappled with the third road agent, wresting his rifle out of his hands.

He discharged the rifle, further spooking the man. This gave Slocum the chance to get a new round in the chamber and fire point-blank into the road agent's gut.

"He shot me."

"Them's cavalry! The varmint was tellin' the truth! He's working for the Army!" The other two raced for cover.

Slocum fired after them but was hindered by his tied feet. He swiveled around, hunting for the gang leader, but Ray Sanders had already lit out. The sound of pounding hooves told Slocum he had missed his chance to stop the owlhoot.

He flopped about on the ground and fired repeatedly after the two outlaws on the run. Slocum missed them by a country mile, but until the cavalry rode up, he kept them back in the wooded area where they had hidden their horses.

At the head of the column, next to an Army major, rode a smiling Helen Murchison.

"What's the matter, John?" she asked, seeing that his feet were still bound. "Did you want to keep from straying?"

"There're two of the gang over yonder," Slocum said, pointing. "And this one needs tending real quick." The third outlaw, the one he had shot in the belly, continued to moan and thrash about weakly.

"I see you have everything in control," she said. "You just wanted to give them a fighting chance, so you tied yourself up."

"Something like that," Slocum said as the major sent a squad after the two fleeing road agents.

Slocum realized how much he had missed her when Helen laughed.

Then the feeling died, and he knew he had unfinished business. Ray Sanders had galloped off before the cavalry even saw him.

18

"We rounded all of them up, Miss Murchison," the major said. He eyed Slocum suspiciously, as if wanting to add him to the roster of shackled prisoners.

"Not all, Major," the dark-haired woman said, chewing her lower lip. "How many are left, John?"

"Can't rightly say, other than the leader. I'd guess there are at least four who are still on the loose. I'm not sure where they were."

"Probably guarding the gold they stole," the officer said sourly.

Slocum hesitated, then asked, "What are you going to do about Blue Claw?"

"I'm sure the Crow will kick up a fuss and draw attention to themselves real soon now. It won't be a matter of finding Blue Claw as much as him finding our settlers," Helen said before the major could answer. "From the expression on your face, John, I suspect you were going to ask about someone else."

"Captain Kernberg," said Slocum. "He's as crooked as a dog's hind leg."

"We know," the major said, looking even surlier. "He used to be a friend."

"Did Welkin spill his guts?" asked Slocum, not sure who would answer. He looked to Helen, who nodded silently.

"We'll round up the captain and anyone else who has been helping him sell firearms to scoundrels like Welkin," said the cavalry officer.

"I've got a score to settle with Ray Sanders," Slocum said. "I'd be obliged if you'd let me bring him in myself. He's only got a short head start."

"Major," started Helen, reaching over and laying her hand on the man's arm. "John deserves this. Please let him go after Sanders."

"He—"

"He *is* an agent for Wells Fargo," Helen said. Slocum tried not to look too surprised that the major swallowed this, hook, line and sinker.

"I see," he major said, stroking his stubbled chin. "Very well. We will bring along these three and hunt for their camp, then arrest Captain Kernberg. Go on, sir," he said to Slocum. "Sanders is all yours."

"Thanks," Slocum said, wondering if he directed this to Helen or the major. It hardly mattered because Helen pulled him to her and kissed him, much to the dismay of the officer. Such public displays were not done in polite society.

"Take Sanders to Moab when you run him to ground," Helen said. "I'll meet you there when we have the situation better in hand."

"Riordan will appreciate having Old Pete's killer locked up," Slocum said. He found his six-shooter in the dirt and spent a few minutes cleaning it. When he found Ray Sanders, he didn't want it jamming on him.

The outlaw leader had made no effort to hide his tracks, choosing speed over stealth. And this was what brought him to the end of his trail. Slocum trotted after Sanders for several miles before seeing the man on foot in the middle of the grassy valley, valiantly struggling to carry his saddlebags and rifle.

Slocum slowed when he saw that Sanders's horse had stepped in a prairie dog hole and broken its leg. Rather than shoot it to put the horse out of its misery, Sanders had cut its throat. The rush of blood had brought ants and scavengers in droves. Slocum gave the horse a wide berth and came up on Sanders from the side.

He had hoped the road agent was too intent on hoofing it to notice a rider to one side, but he was wrong. Ray Sanders was like a sensitive, throbbing tooth. The slightest movement upset him. The outlaw spotted Slocum when he was hardly closer than a hundred yards.

Sanders grunted, dropped his saddlebags and fell belly down on the ground, using the saddlebags to steady his rifle. He began firing methodically at Slocum, taking his time like he was shooting at tin cans on a fence post.

"Give up, Sanders. You can't get away. All your men are prisoners, and the cavalry's after Kernberg." Slocum yanked out the Winchester from his sheath but knew there was an advantage being without a horse. Sanders could shoot until Slocum was also on foot. Without putting too fine an edge on it, Slocum guessed those saddlebags were filled with ammunition.

In a lengthy fight, Sanders would come out on top.

Bullets flew around Slocum's head and spooked his horse. He thought about dismounting, then knew the horse was his only advantage. With a rebel yell, Slocum put his spurs to the horse's flanks and rocketed toward Sanders. This was the last thing in the world the outlaw expected. He hesitated for a moment and gave Slocum a chance to get closer.

Mounted, Slocum looked down on the prone road agent. Gripping the horse with his strong knees, Slocum began firing as fast as he could as he galloped forward.

One of his shots was luckier than it was accurate, hitting a stone in front of Sanders and ricocheting upward into the man's face.

Sanders dropped his rifle to claw at his eyes—and then Slocum was on him. Diving from horseback, Slocum landed smack on top of the outlaw. Which man was in greater pain as a result was something Slocum didn't want to consider. The beating Sanders and his men had given him came back double now in every bruise and ache on his body, but Slocum managed to drive the butt of his rifle into the center of Sanders's back.

This drove the man down. And he stayed.

Panting, Slocum got to his feet, steadied himself, then kicked the other rifle away where Sanders couldn't reach it.

"Get on your feet. We've got a ways to go."

"Where?" Sanders clawed at his eyes to get the dirt and rock dust out. "Where are you taking me?"

"First, we're going to fetch the gold you stole. Then we're going back to Moab so the marshal can put you in that fine lockup of his."

"First, you're going to hell!" snarled Sanders.

Slocum aimed his rifle at the man but Sanders didn't flinch.

"The gold you stole," Slocum said. "Where is it? I can leave your carcass out here for the buzzards easier than I can take you in for the law to deal with."

"Kill me and you'll never find the gold."

Slocum frowned, trying to remember something that had occurred to him earlier, but it slipped away like sand through his fingers. It was almost as if he knew where Sanders had hidden the gold from the stagecoach robbery, but that was ridiculous. The outlaw had never told Slocum any such thing.

"I'd get the pleasure of watching you die," Slocum said. He sucked in a deep breath and felt hot pain lance into his body to remind him of what Sanders had done to him.

"But you'd never find the gold. None of my men know where I put it. Any of it."

"Even the gold from Blue Claw?" Slocum thought Sanders was lying.

"You killed the only other one of my gang who knew."

"Marley," Slocum said. "Was that why the others hated him so?"

"He was a son of a bitch, and they hated him before we hid the gold. I let him come to help hide the gold since I knew the others would never trust him. If he crossed me, they'd kill him."

"It's a long walk to Moab," Slocum said. "Might be you'll decide to talk before we get there." He swung his rifle around and pointed in the direction of the town. "Be glad I'm letting you keep your boots."

Sanders grumbled under his breath, cursing Slocum. He climbed to his feet and started to pick up the saddlebags.

Slocum fired a round through the leather, knocking the saddlebags from the road agent's hands. Without saying a word, Slocum went over and nudged open a flap. Inside were two six-shooters and more ammo than he could shake a stick at.

"Start walking, unless you'd like to run."

Sanders muttered some more but began trudging in the direction Slocum indicated. It took Slocum a spell to find the Colorado River and get his bearings, but when he did, he knew where to find Moab. Three days later they marched into town. Sanders was footsore but still close-mouthed about where he had hidden the gold stolen from Wells Fargo.

Slocum was aware of how the townspeople slipped indoors to watch the small parade as he herded the outlaw toward Marshal Yarrow's calaboose. A prickly feeling rose on the back of his neck as he remembered that these were the people who had wanted to string him up.

"What we got here?" asked Yarrow, coming from his jailhouse. The marshal had his thumbs hooked into his gun belt.

"Brought you the man who killed Old Pete and the passengers and stole the gold," Slocum said. "This is Ray Sanders."

"Do tell," Yarrow said, stepping out of the doorway into the street. He stood as if he intended to throw down on Slocum, his hand resting on the side of his holster now. Slocum wondered if the marshal could be that stupid. Even on horseback, Slocum could draw and fire before the lawman could clear leather.

"You probably have a wanted poster or two on him."

Sanders spoke up. "I don't know what this cayuse is saying. I was minding my own business, he shoots my horse out from under me and makes me walk here and threatened to kill me if I tried to get away."

"Shut up, Sanders. Slocum's right about one thing. I *do* have a wanted poster on you from over in Colorado. You've been on a real spree."

"I didn't do anything here in Utah," protested Sanders.

"Shut up," Slocum said, kicking the man and sending him stumbling in the direction of the jailhouse door.

"Think you'd better take your own advice, Slocum." Yarrow's shoulders squared and the marshal's hand twitched slightly. "You escaped my lockup, and that's a crime. And I ain't so sure you're blameless in killing the driver and passengers, not to mention swipin' all that gold."

"Miss Murchison told you—"

"Don't much know about that little lady, either. A couple folks think they saw someone looking a lot like her helpin' you escape. Any woman that purty gets noticed, no matter how much she tries to hide her face and figure."

"Sanders is the guilty party. Him and his gang." Slocum

had started to tell Marshal Yarrow that an Army company was rounding up the rest of the outlaws when he heard a pair of clicks that caused him to look over his shoulder.

A deputy stood at the corner of the jail sighting down the long barrels of a shotgun. The sound Slocum had heard was the deputy pulling back both hammers on the double-barreled gun.

"You're gonna get splattered all over the street if you don't lose that rifle and your six-shooter, Slocum," said Yarrow. "Even if you can nail Fred there, you got me to contend with."

The marshal tensed when he saw the storm cloud crossing Slocum's face. For two cents Slocum would take out the marshal and still probably get the deputy.

"There's a couple more boys out there. Look around, Slocum, 'fore you do anything dumb that'll get you killed." Yarrow pointed down Moab's main street.

Slocum saw a man with a rifle poking his head out the second story of the mercantile. Another braced his rifle against the rickety porch railing of a bookstore. A third man farther down came from inside the hotel and hurried into the middle of the street. From the way his hands shook, the man was more dangerous to Yarrow than Slocum if he opened fire, but the number of guns pointed at him decided Slocum. Too much lead flying meant innocent bystanders would be hurt.

Worse, Sanders was likely to slip away in the confusion.

"All right, Marshal, but you're making a big mistake."

"That's what you said before, Slocum. I know a desperado when I see one. Toss Fred there your rifle and drop your six-gun." Yarrow openly gloated now because he had recaptured the only man to escape jail while he was marshal.

Ray Sanders laughed nastily at Slocum's predicament.

"Put us in the same cell," Slocum said. "If you have to lock me up, put me in the same cell as Sanders." Seeing the outlaw turn pale at the idea of being caged with Slocum was almost worth being locked up. Almost.

19

Ray Sanders sat huddled on the far side of his cell, as far away from the shared bars between his and Slocum's as he could get. He had taken it to heart what Slocum had said about wanting to be locked up with him.

"You'll never find the gold," Sanders said, taunting Slocum. "Even if you don't rot in this hellhole, you'll never get the gold." Sanders looked quickly in the direction of Yarrow's office to be sure the marshal wasn't eavesdropping.

Slocum stared at the outlaw, the niggling sensation telling him how wrong that was about finding the gold. Somehow, Sanders had already told him where the stolen shipment was, and Slocum just couldn't put his finger on it. A word, a hint, a look—something had given the gunrunner away, but Slocum was at a loss to figure it out right now.

"They'll hang you, you know," Sanders said, louder now that he had seen Yarrow moving around in the office. He had an audience to play for. "You killed Old Pete and the other two."

"I'll be at your execution, Ray," Slocum said. He kept his voice level because he knew that would scare Sanders the most. Ranting, raving, drawing attention to himself was what the outlaw wanted, knowing such reaction would further incriminate Slocum with the lawman. Slocum held the whip hand and wanted Sanders to know it. "I'll be there as a witness. There's too much evidence against you."

"What evidence? Your word?" Sanders laughed harshly. "The marshal tossed you in the hoosegow the instant he laid eyes on you. The only reason he's keeping me is that he doesn't know you did it all! You robbed the stage and killed those people."

"Welkin has spilled his guts by now," Slocum said.

"Welkin," scoffed Sanders. "What's that lamebrained son of a bitch know, anyway?"

Again Slocum had the uneasy feeling he was missing some clue to unlocking the mystery of the hidden gold. Welkin wouldn't know. He hadn't been part of Sanders's gang—he had only been a go-between so Captain Kernberg would never know who was selling the guns to the Indians.

"How much do you figure you stole, Ray?" Slocum asked in a conversational tone. "From what Riordan said, you got sixteen thousand dollars in gold coin off the Wells Fargo shipment. How much did Blue Claw pay you for the stolen Army rifles? You never paid Welkin. In fact, you intended to swindle him out of his due, you and Sergeant Tompkins. Maybe you thought you'd kill both of them and erase all the witnesses against you."

"You've been smoking loco weed," Sanders said, his eyes darting toward the half-open door leading to the marshal's office. Yarrow crossed their line of sight as he went to the door when the bell jangled. Slocum had not expected Sanders to confess, but he had hoped the man would brag a mite and give another clue to the whereabouts of the gold.

"Got another one to keep you company, boys," Marshal Yarrow said.

"Hello, John," Helen Murchison said.

"Come to get me out?" he asked. Then he saw that the marshal had his six-shooter aimed at Helen's back.

"Oh, you and I'll be on our way before you know it. Never fear," she said. "This is all a big mistake that Marshal Yarrow will realize soon enough."

"Don't count on it, Missy. You busted that varmint out of my jail. I got witnesses. You're as big a crook as he is, though I gotta admit you're a durn sight purtier."

"The Army's not going to like you imprisoning me or Mr. Slocum," Helen said.

"What's she going on about?" Sanders jumped to his feet and gripped the broad steel straps of his jail cell.

"She works for the Department of War," Slocum said. "She's got Welkin in custody up in Salt Lake City where they're sweating the truth out of him."

"You folks surely do spin a wild tale. In you go, little lady." Yarrow had started to push Helen into a third cell when he stepped away to see who had barreled into his office. The bell on the door clanged furiously and the floorboards creaked under the heavy weight as men crowded in.

"What'n the hell's goin' on out there?" demanded the marshal. "Who are you?" Any hint of satisfaction faded from Yarrow like snow in the spring sun when he saw a sea of blue uniforms, dangling sabers and an acre of gold braid.

"The cavalry's arrived," Helen said, smiling.

"Yes, sir, Slocum, never doubted you for a minute. After what Miss Murchison has to say 'bout you, why Wells Fargo ought to give you a medal. 'Cept they don't do nuthing like that," Gus Riordan said. The Wells Fargo agent turned glum. "Wish you could have brought back the gold. Course, it's fine you got Old Pete's killers. But findin' the gold woulda been nice."

"The cavalry will be taking Sanders and the rest of his gang off Marshal Yarrow's hands soon," Helen Murchison said. "Gunrunning is a serious crime, but not as serious as stealing the rifles from the Army in the first place."

"Sanders has a powerful lot to answer for," Slocum said, a distant look in his eyes. The answer to his question floated just beyond his grasp, tantalizing him like a mirage in the middle of a desert does a man dying of thirst.

"You've got your job back, if you want it, Slocum," Riordan said. "Sorry 'bout all the confusion. Didn't mean to imply, earlier that is, that I thought you was a killer or anything like that. Still, the gold. Losin' it means Wells Fargo will move the depot to Green River, and this ole town's gonna dry up and blow away. A real shame, that."

"Never give up hope, Mr. Riordan," Helen said. "Sanders might hand over the gold if he thinks he can get a lighter sentence."

"Lighter sentence or longer rope?" joked the stagecoach agent. "Ain't no way that owlhoot will escape the hangman's noose, no matter what he says or does."

"I'll let you know about riding shotgun for you," Slocum said. "First, I have some business to tend to."

"You've got a job as long as the depot's here, Slocum. Yes, sir, you're one of the best I ever hired." Riordan bustled off to talk to a reporter from Salt Lake City who had gotten wind of the gunrunners being captured.

"Let's go, John," Helen said. "I know that reporter fellow, and he can talk the ear off a cornstalk."

They walked down the street, heading for the hotel where Helen had taken a room.

"You look distracted," she said, her blue eyes shining. "I have just the medicine to do something about perking you up. Way up," the dark-haired beauty said, her hand brushing across Slocum's crotch.

"Who am I to say no when I've been locked up in the marshal's jail?" Slocum said, grinning. They went up the stairs to the second-floor hotel room. Before Slocum had the door closed behind them, Helen was shedding her garments.

"It is a warmish day, isn't it? Why don't you get comfortable, too?"

She watched as he stripped off his dusty, dirty clothes and kicked them into a pile on the floor. "My, my," she said, her eyes fixed on his groin. "I'm glad to see you have *something* on. Something nice and hard, too."

"Just for you," Slocum said. "But it's not too comfortable."

"I can make it . . . exciting," Helen said in a husky voice.

She moved to him like a shadow crossing a wall, but no shadow was ever so sexually insistent, so loving with its kisses, so resolute with the way she took him in hand. Helen stroked up and down his engorged length until Slocum feared he would lose control like a young buck with his first woman.

Helen sensed his intense arousal and suddenly turned from him and stood, her hands grabbing the brass rail at the foot of the bed. She widened her stance and rose onto tiptoe, then waggled her perky rump in his direction.

"See anything you like, John?" she teased.

He stepped up, reaching around her so he could cup her dangling teats. Squeezing down gently produced just the reaction he sought. A delicate shiver passed through the woman's lush body and caused her to shove her rear end backward into the curve of his groin. Slocum abandoned one firm breast with its throbbingly hard nip, stroked across the woman's heaving belly and then went further.

He found the tangled dark mat of the furry triangle snuggled between her legs. His finger stabbed out, pushed aside the pinkly scalloped flaps and then entered her up to the second knuckle of his middle finger. Helen gasped again and tossed back her head like a frisky filly waiting to be ridden.

"More, John. I want something more in me. Something bigger. Something like this!" She groped between her own legs and caught at his rigid pole bouncing behind her. Tugging gently, she guided it for the spot where his finger moved with deceptive slowness in and out of her steamy interior. When she brushed away his hand, he moved it to the delicate vee of her nether lips and began stroking over a tiny button of flesh he found there. At the same time, he felt the heat boiling from inside her, along the entire length of his manhood.

Slocum levered forward and sank deep into the woman's most intimate recess. She shrieked in joy, then began grinding her hips back to take even more of him into her. The corkscrewing motion thrilled Slocum, but he needed more. So did Helen.

He began retreating and advancing, slowly at first, then with more speed and determination until he was slamming hard and fast into her from behind. He felt her fleshy buttocks flatten against his hard belly as he strove to slip his meaty shaft ever deeper into her. A lewd sucking sound filled the room to give testimony to the force and rapidity of his movements in her constricting, moist female sheath.

Crying out in wanton joy, Helen shuddered all over. Slocum felt her tightness clamp down on his hidden length even more, milking him. He kept thrusting, burning as he went into her liquid depths, and then he wasn't able to hold back anymore. Heat from the delightful carnal friction burned away his control faster and faster. The tide built deep in his loins and reached the point where the pressure was impossible to contain. Slocum surged forward and exploded deep inside her, setting off another bout of pure lust in the woman.

They rocked back and forth together and then the sensations died within him. He sagged forward, his hairy chest resting against her back. He reached under her and toyed with her nipples and stroked over her belly.

"You want more, John? I do!"

"You're insatiable," he accused.

"I'm in heat!" she cried as she straightened up.

Helen swung about in the circle of his arms and kissed him flush on the lips. Her body undulated against him, like a kitten stroking itself against a human's leg. Her roving hand tangled in the hair on his chest before it wandered down and found his limpness. She pushed back slightly, looked up at him and *tsk-tsk-tsk*'d disapprovingly.

"And I thought you wanted me again. I see that I have to do something about this sorry state."

She dropped to her knees and applied herself to restoring him to his former vigor. Her lips sucked and kissed, then she began licking the entire underside of the slowly stiffening stalk. Slocum was surprised at how quickly he was ready for her again.

Through the hot summer afternoon and into the cool evening they made love; then with the woman sleeping contentedly beside him in bed, Slocum sat up.

"Of course," he said. "Sanders was a sharp character, but he couldn't think fast enough to come up with anything really clever." Slocum started to wake Helen, then decided against it. He fetched his clothes and quickly donned them. As he left the room, he strapped on his gun belt.

He had gold to find. And he thought he knew where to find it.

*   *   *

A little past noon on the second day after leaving Moab, Slocum reached the Colorado River. He got his bearings, decided where Sanders and his gang had camped and where he had tried to bamboozle them into believing he was another gunrunner, then headed south along the river. The day's heat faded along with the bright sun, and a chilly breeze whipped down the canyon by the time he reached an oxbow in the river.

This was the spot Sanders had chosen to meet to swap gold for the rifles intended for the Navajo. Slocum reined back and stood in the stirrups, studying the sandy area of the oxbow. The river had curved over the years, almost leaving an island pinched off in the middle of the water. Almost.

Sanders had come up with the spot fast. Too fast. While Sanders might have chosen this oxbow because he knew it for other reasons, Slocum decided the outlaw leader had known about it because this was where he had buried the gold. Since the gold was on his mind more than any deal for another shipment of stolen rifles, this location had slipped out.

Sanders hadn't been too uneasy about it because he knew Slocum wasn't a gunrunner and he intended to kill Slocum after he learned who else was working with him.

"Big spot," Slocum said to himself, looking around the area. It was a powerful lot of sand and dirt to dig in aimlessly. There had to be some way for Sanders to find the loot easily.

Slocum decided against searching the shoreline. The drought had caused the river to fall a couple feet. In a season with normal runoff, any such hiding place would be underwater and Sanders would run the risk of having the gold washed away by the powerful current.

Likewise, a good year for runoff would lift the Colorado another couple feet all around the sandy spit. Although Sanders didn't intend to leave the gold buried that long, Slocum felt the road agent was a cautious man—when it came to preserving his hoard of gold.

Looking over the barren terrain didn't give any clear indication of where the treasure might be. A few struggling cottonwoods, some low scrubby bushes, stretches of buffalo grass, and growing shadows that made hunting for anything more difficult by the minute were the most prominent features. Slocum dismounted and began searching in a crisscross pattern until twilight turned to night. He finally gave up when it became too dark to see without a lantern. Throwing in the sponge and abandoning his hunt for the night, Slocum pitched camp, fixed supper and thought hard about Sanders.

He fell asleep with visions of gold dancing in his head, only to come suddenly awake at dawn. Whether it was a dream or real, Slocum couldn't tell, but a neighing horse had brought him out of his fitful sleep. He yawned, stretched and sat up. The sun poked over the distant rim of the canyon so a single ray raked across the oxbow as straight as an arrow.

"That's it," Slocum decided, forgetting about the horse in his dreams. He jumped to his feet and put his back to the sun, so he was looking along the solitary ray shining between two rock needles on the distant rim. A broad grin came to his lips when a dazzling reflection almost blinded him.

He hurried to the spot and found a silver dollar jammed into the crook of a dead tree branch. The wood had then been driven into the soft ground like a grave marker. Slocum doubted he would find a dead body as he started digging. Quite the contrary. He expected to find gold.

It took longer than he expected to scrabble through the sand, dirt and rock, but he soon grasped the edge of a heavy, stitched sack. He tugged on it but the sack remained pinned down. Throwing dirt in all directions like a dog digging for a buried bone, he unearthed the canvas mailbag that had been carried under Old Pete's feet on the Wells Fargo stage. Slocum dragged it out and flopped the heavy sack onto the ground beside him.

"Got it," he said in satisfaction. Slocum dumped the contents out onto the ground and sorted through them, putting gold coins in one stack and gold jewelry and other trinkets in the other.

A quick count showed almost $16,000 in coins. The Wells Fargo loot. And the rest, an impressive pile almost twice that stolen from the stage company, had to be the ill-gotten gains Blue Claw had paid for the rifles.

Slocum sat and stared and thought hard. He had been through hell. His name was cleared in Moab of both murder and robbery, for whatever that was worth, and Riordan had guaranteed him a job when he returned. But this was a powerful lot of money. He could ride shotgun messenger for the rest of his life and not make this much.

Slocum heaved a deep sigh and began putting it back into the heavy canvas bag. All of it.

He hoisted it to his shoulder, staggered under the load, then went to where his horse grazed peacefully on a small patch of buffalo grass. The horse protested mightily when he loaded the gold onto its back.

Slocum saw the way the horse bowed under the weight and knew he should have brought a pack mule with him. There was nothing he could do about that now. Slocum packed his gear, slung it behind the gold and started back to Moab, walking.

Before he had gone a mile, he heard a horse ahead of him. Slocum reached down and made sure his six-shooter rode easy in its holster. After he had decided to return the gold, he should have left the stolen loot where it was and returned with Riordan and a half dozen of the cavalry troopers to guard it on the way back to Moab. He wasn't sure how many of Sanders's gang might still be on the loose. He hadn't paid enough attention to identifying the road agents, and now he might pay the price for his lapse.

The sound of the approaching horse caused him to ease his six-gun from its holster. He held it at his side, ready for the shootout he expected to come.

"Top of the morning, John," came Helen's cheery greeting.

He didn't say anything for a moment. He had left her without a word of explanation, but she wasn't visibly upset.

"What brings you out here?" he asked.

"You worried me, just for a while, John. I woke up and you had hightailed it from Moab, so I had to follow."

"You did a good job. Until your horse woke me making a racket this morning."

"I wondered if you had heard. I was watching you while you slept." Helen reached behind and pulled a spyglass. "Oh, don't get upset. I didn't sneak up on you. I was halfway up the hill yonder."

"I found all the gold."

"From the Wells Fargo robbery? The stage we rode?"

"That and the trinkets Blue Claw swapped for his rifles."

"You're returning it all?" Helen studied him closely. He said nothing. "I thought so. You have an honest streak in you, John. You are a continual surprise to me. I like that in a man."

"You want to ride back with me? I can use a guard, especially one as good with a rifle as you are."

"There isn't a reward for the Wells Fargo shipment," she said.

Slocum shrugged it off.

"Why are you returning it? You could have ridden off with a fortune."

"You'd have tracked me to the ends of the earth," Slocum said.

"Is that so bad?" Helen laughed. "You didn't know

anyone was out here. No, John, you decided to go back to Moab before you knew I was following."

"I've got a question," Slocum said. "You work for the Department of War. How'd that come about?" He saw her face become a mask. Then the expression softened a mite as she answered.

"My husband was attached to the inspector general's office. He found out about gunrunning—someone else, not Kernberg or Sanders and Welkin—and it got him killed. The IG asked if I would finish the job Aaron had started. I did and it felt good, damned good. I decided to give it another try when I heard about Kernberg ordering such heavy ordnance for a simple scout. Bringing men like that to justice has its rewards."

"Not unlike pinning the murder and robbery charges on Ray Sanders, and returning what he stole," Slocum said.

"We're alike in that respect, John. I'm glad we are so different in others."

Slocum kept walking. Helen turned her pony's face and rode slowly beside him.

"I can take the Wells Fargo gold back for you. It'll save the town when the company builds the new depot, and your duty will be done."

"What about the rest of the gold? It was stolen by the Crow."

"Stolen from dead settlers, mostly," Helen said. "There's nobody to return it to. If you kept it as your reward, I wouldn't put up a fuss about it."

Slocum looked at her, then said, "I hear something more in your voice. What is it?"

"Why, John, whatever could a poor low-paid, soon to be former employee of the War Department do if you just upped and went to Denver? What could I *ever* do if you checked into the Metropole Hotel—I like it better than the Brown Palace—and just happened to have a big, soft bed in the room? You could wait a week or two and see who turned up."

"Is there a good restaurant in the Metropole?" Slocum asked.

"I don't know," Helen Murchison said, grinning ear to ear. "I seldom leave the room. And you won't either, after I get there."

"I won't wait forever," Slocum said, pulling the heavy canvas sack from horseback to divvy the loot so he could take the part from Blue Claw and Helen could return the Wells Fargo shipment.

His words caused her to sit straighter in the saddle.

"I wouldn't wait more than a year or two," Slocum said. It was his turn to smile.

"I'll be there before you can kick off your boots," Helen Murchison assured him.

And she was.

Watch for

SLOCUM AND THE BOUNTY JUMPERS

291st novel in the exciting SLOCUM series
from Jove

Coming in May!